City of Stone

F.L.Rose

Published by F.L.Rose, 2023.

This is a work of fiction. Similarities to real people, places, or events are entirely coincidental.

CITY OF STONE

First edition. April 12, 2023.

Copyright © 2023 F.L.Rose.

ISBN: 979-8215708514

Written by F.L.Rose.

Table of Contents

City of Stone

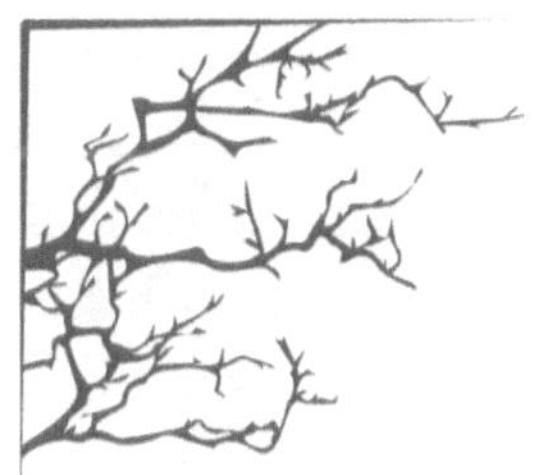

I first came to the City of Stone – Gjirokastre, Albania - on business. I was working as an agent for a firm looking to invest in real estate in Albania, which was at that time only just opening up after her long experiment with communism. Of course I went first to the coastal areas near the Greek island of Corfu, as these were the most accessible to tourists, but already the price of property there was rising, and so my employers asked me to visit some of the inland cities where they had heard there was potential for future tourism.

I drove to Gjirokastre in the old Fiat I had hired in Sarande, and almost immediately got myself into a most embarrassing situation. I should mention here that Gjirokastre is an ancient city, around twenty kilometres from the sea as the crow flies but more or less set into the side of a high mountain range – almost every building, at least in the old part, is built of the grey, pink, white and black stones that may be found in the region. Even the roofs are built of it. When it rains, so I'm told, the stones glisten silver in the wet, and unwary walkers go sliding down the streets on their backsides. So it is also called, besides the City of Stone, the Silver City.

In any case, unfamiliar with the steep and ill-maintained streets, I tried to drive up to my accommodation – a hotel ensconced high on the hill – and went a little too fast and careless. Halfway up I hit a hole in the road full of sharpened paving stones and with a loud pop my front tyre went flat.

I got out to look at the damage, and it seemed to me that half the population of the town gathered within seconds and began to offer advice and commentary. Since it was all in Albanian it was lost on me, but they seemed helpful – particularly when I found that there was no spare tyre in the boot nor equipment for removing the wheel. A barrel-shaped Albanian man came bustling out from his house, took one look at the problem and with gestures and smiles indicated that he could conjure a replacement tyre for me from somewhere in the area – and within half an hour he had, and the car was roadworthy again.

It was in this way that I met my first friend in Albania. He was a cheerful family man named Amar and that night he invited me home for dinner with his wife and three teenage children and told me all about the city and its history. "We have fallen on hard times here," he said, "since the end of the war and the Communists, but Ali Pasha once held that fortress up there, and we were famous for our silver and goldsmithing. There are still some very fine houses to be seen, although the owners can hardly afford to live in them since Hoxha took all their money away."

"Yes," said his wife, Eva, "they call them the fortified houses. The old families were always fighting with one another and so they built great walls around their houses and gates that could be defended against each other in time of war. Those were the days of blood feuds, when the killings could go on and on for generations – thank God at least Hoxha put an end to that."

Hoxha, you'll recall, was Albania's dictator for forty years after the war, and was now much loathed by almost everyone.

As it turned out, there was a lot of vacant property in the city which was both attractive and cheap, and so I stayed there for a number of weeks, negotiating on behalf of my firm. While I was there I deepened my friendship with Amar and his family and got to know the Gjirokastrians a little better. It was very much a man's town, on the face of it – the bars were full of men, and old men would congregate wherever there was a flat space, a park or a bench, calling out to one another as they strolled past. It was clear that most people had known each other all their lives.

Which is why it was all the more strange when I was taking an evening stroll with Amar and some of his friends under the great grey walls of the castle and we passed an elderly lady, supported by her grand-daughter (or so I guessed) coming slowly the other way. The older woman was dressed, as many are here, in a black short sleeved dress, her silver hair elegantly confined in a bun. She was slim and fine-featured, but it was the girl I really noticed.

She was not particularly pretty, but from the first I was mesmerised. Like most young Albanian women she wore her hair long, flowing to the waist; in the evening dimness it seemed as black as the darkness behind the closed door of a cellar. Her face was narrow and angular, and her cheekbones stood out sharply under the smooth olive skin. But her lips were as full as over-ripe figs, and she had an absolute self-possession that struck me almost as a force, quivering through the air between us. And her eyes – they were light grey, slanted, and brilliant as a wolf's.

"Who are they?" I asked Amar. "That woman and the girl?"

He and his friends exchanged glances. "No idea," he said after a pause, and I knew he was lying. "Probably some tourist from the south."

I raised my eyebrows. "Really? They don't look like tourists."

He shrugged. "Perhaps from Greece or Bosnia, who can tell?" and seemed to quicken his pace.

The next day I made a point of walking under the castle walls on my own, and sure enough I saw the old lady sedately strolling along, her hand on the arm of the lithe girl beside her. I gathered all my courage together – telling myself they could only ignore me, at worst – and went to introduce myself.

"I'm Richard Temple," I said, stepping in front of the girl so that she had to pause in her walking, "and my friends tell me you are strangers here, like me, so I thought I'd stop and say hello."

The grandmother smiled graciously; the girl looked at me silently with those light unreadable eyes.

"Strangers?" said the old lady. "Who told you that? My family have lived here for a thousand years. I hardly think that makes us strangers."

I began to apologise, explaining that I'd been misinformed, but she waved her hand. "It doesn't matter. I am Princess Maria, and this is my grand-daughter Arjuna, and we are both pleased to meet you, aren't we Arjuna?"

She explained, as we walked along, that she was the last scion of the ancient royal family of Gjirokaster, but that they had lost all their lands and wealth under Communism – in fact, she herself had only narrowly escaped execution as an enemy of the state. "I don't stand on my rank," she said haughtily, "for we are all equals now, but it is in the nature of people to resent us for what we were once. They can't help it."

That went some way to explaining Amar's peculiar lie. I have to admit I was a little overawed by the revelation that I was speaking to genuine European royalty – and of such antiquity. However much of an anachronism they might be these days, I couldn't help a visceral response of respect and admiration.

The next day, and the day after that, I deliberately chose to keep company with the Princess and her grand-daughter rather than with Amar and his friends. He was a little hurt, I could tell, but the Princess didn't seem to mind; in fact she beckoned me to her as soon as she saw me and positively encouraged me to stay by them. The girl said nothing but her luminous eyes seemed to appraise me in the twilight, as if weighing my intentions towards them.

After about a week, Amar trotted up to me in the street, looking worried, and drew me aside.

"I see that you're walking out with the Princess..."

"Oh so you do know who she is?" I said with a grin. "Why didn't you tell me when I asked?"

He looked uncomfortable. "Because – because I have come to like you very much, Richard, and I do not think these people are good company for you."

How odd, I thought. "Why not?"

"They are not your kind."

"What do you mean?"

"The fly should not make friends with the spider."

I laughed, a little shocked. "Are you calling that nice old lady a spider?"

"Her and the girl," Stan pronounced, his cheerful face in unaccustomed lines of disapproval, "are vermin. They are like cockroaches – we try to get rid of them but still they come back to scuttle under our floorboards."

I was startled at his vehemence. I had no idea that he harboured such strong anti-royalist feelings, but I suppose the legacy of Communism had left deeper marks than I knew. I was indignant, also, on the Princess's behalf; she had been nothing but kind and gracious to me. And the girl – the truth is that I was already in love with her.

He had given me no good reason not to associate with the couple, but even if he had done, I would have taken no notice at that point. So instead of withdrawing from their company I actually redoubled my efforts to get to know them, and in particular Arjuna. I was very conscious that in a short time I would have to go back to France, where my employers were, and then who knows when I would see her again?

Matters progressed well, to the extent that the old lady would slow her step and drop behind, to allow Arjuna and I to walk together in the dusk. We talked about life in France – Arjuna had never left the stone city – and about the family's trials under Communism, and eventually I asked if I could call on them at their home. I had in mind that I would make a formal proposal of marriage to Arjuna with her mother present. So entrapped was I already by the power of her presence!

Arjuna seemed to feel for me something at least of what I felt for her – so I interpreted the brilliant, focused intensity of her gaze – but I thought that I had a better chance if I approached this the old fashioned way, given their royal status and traditional comportment.

"Home?" said the Princess, when I raised it. "Oh, I'm afraid we live in a dreadful ruin. I would be ashamed to invite you there."

When she said this, I took it as a polite indication that it had been forward of me to ask, and couldn't help looking a little downcast, but Arjuna, with a glance from her crystal eyes, stepped in.

"My grandmother is telling nothing but the truth. We live in a ruin. But you're welcome to visit us there, if you wish." And she gave me an address and a time – somewhat late in the evening, but then Albanians like most Mediterranean peoples stay up very late at night and are slow to rise in the mornings.

So the next night I found my way to the address given – and stood troubled and confused. For it was, literally and unexpectedly, a ruin. It had once, I could see, been a large and stately house, perhaps even a palace. It was set high up on the mountain, overlooking the valley, and had stout stone walls and a high iron gate. This in itself wasn't unusual – as I mentioned, many wealthy old houses here were fortified as of old, against the Turk or rival families. But, pushing open the rusted gate, I could hardly see how the place could be inhabited at all. The roof was missing, the windows gaped, missing all but a few shards of glass, and rubble and rubbish littered the broken mosaic tiles of the outer courtyard.

I stood uncertainly in the ornate, crumbling gateway, and then to my relief Arjuna appeared. She was alone, and did not seem in the least abashed by my discovery of the squalor in which – could it be true? – they lived.

"You came," she stated coolly. "Well, now you see what we've come to, we who used to be rulers of this place."

So saying, she led me in over the broken tiles and through the doorless entry – guarded by blackened gargoyles, down a set of crumbling, ancient stairs, and at last, when I was thinking that the two of them must sleep amongst the stray cats that stalked amid the rubbish, mewling, into an inner chamber, black as ink. She lit a lantern

– evidently the place had no electricity – and by the illumination I saw two mattresses laid out on the stone floor, and a black dress hung on a nail in a corner.

"My grandmother is out," she explained, in the tone of someone who has brought a friend into a perfectly normal living room, "I hope you don't mind."

"Not at all," I said, "But I'm so sorry to see that you're reduced to living in these circumstances. You should be living like a Queen, with the best that money could buy and yet you are here, in this..."

"Yes," she said calmly, "I would wish better for my grandmother, at her age, but we manage."

For the life of me I could not see how. There was no bathroom – although there was a crumbling well in the courtyard – and no heating for the fiercely cold Albanian winters. How could they maintain themselves? And yet in appearance they were both elegant and in no way unkempt. I didn't know what to say – so after a short silence I just blurted out what had been on my mind, when I set out to visit this peculiar home.

"I don't want you to have to manage. For you, for *anyone* to live in these appalling conditions, it's not right!" She raised her thick dark eyebrows. "And, well, there is something I've been wanting to ask you, Arjuna. I did mean to ask you in the presence of your grandmother but since she isn't here I'll just come out with it. I love you. Will you marry me?"

For answer she swayed close to me, slid her slim, strong arms about my neck and pressed her lips to mine. It was the sweetest, most intoxicating kiss I have ever experienced, as if I had taken some mad, disturbing drug. Almost I felt that some of the power of her – her strange, mesmerising wildness – leaked into me at that moment through the richness of her lips, and I was lost. Before I quite knew what was happening, we had sunk on to one of the mattresses and then she was half-naked beside me, clinging and coiling about me, sinuous in the lantern light...

And then I heard the sound of heavy feet in the rubble, and the shape of a man appeared in the black doorway. Arjuna quickly – but with the grace of a cat – rose to her feet, and I scrambled up beside her, feeling terribly vulnerable and embarrassed. Could this be her father? And if it was, he'd probably react like any red-blooded Albanian patriarch and murder me on the spot!

I could just make out his features – they were strong and handsome, if a little rough-hewn, and he had a great black moustache that curled fiercely over his lip. He seemed too young to be her father, I thought, and then he said,

"Who the fuck are you?" in an accent that wasn't Albanian at all, but perhaps Italian?

I looked at Arjuna, whose eyes were fixed on him in an icy stare.

"What business is it of yours?"

"I'm her fucking husband." He took a threatening step forward, and I prepared to defend myself, but Arjuna glided between us.

"Antonio, leave him."

If I'd been her husband, those words wouldn't have stopped me from punching my rival in the head, but Antonio stopped at once – in fact he froze, as if turned into a stone statue. Only his eyes watched me, with a terrible resentment. Mixed – strangely – with fear.

"I'm sorry, Richard. I can explain," Arjuna said in her harsh yet sibilant voice, and taking my hand she led me out past him, leaving the injured husband standing there like a spellbound bull.

Of course, as soon as we were in the courtyard, I faced her and asked why she had never told me she was married. Since I had never asked, the whole thing was my own fault, really, but I felt I had a right to an explanation. Arjuna, fixing me with those predatory eyes, put a finger on my lips.

"I don't love him," she said, sliding close to me. "He is a nuisance to me now. I wish he were dead. It is you I love."

I pushed her away from me pettishly. "That's all very well but he's not dead and you're married to him and I – I wish you had told me."

She let go of me then, frowning, and before I could say another word, she disappeared like a shadow back into the darkness of the empty, ruined house.

I left, confused and despairing, and on my way back to my hotel I passed Amar's house, and saw that the lights were still on and the door open. I could see Eva, his wife, cooking inside. I followed my urge and knocked on the door.

Eva welcomed me gladly, and set a generous slice of honey cake in front of me and a glass of some strong local liqueur, flavoured with mountain herbs.

"Now what is the matter with you?" she said, sitting down opposite me, "You look like you've fallen down a well."

I was aching for someone to confide in, so I told her all about it – including Arjuna's husband – and she reached forward and clasped my hand in sympathy.

"So you love this girl?"

"More than my life," I said, realising that the cliched words were, in fact, true – I would have gladly died under that glittering gaze.

"Enough to wish a man dead?"

I knew at once what she meant. "To *wish* a man dead, yes, but not to kill him. Even if I could. I'm not a murderer."

She nodded. "So. Let me tell you a secret of that family. You have heard of blood feuds, perhaps? In this country, when a man of one family kills a man of another, or rapes a girl, then the other family must kill or rape in return. For a thousand years this has been the custom, and for most of those years, the family of Arjuna has ruled over us. It so happened that many centuries ago a prince of the royal family raped a girl from one of the other noble families, and so the head of that family swore to rape the royal princess in return and slaughter her brothers to avenge her honour. The royal princess at that time was called Arjuna – it is a family name – and she went of her own accord to the head of that other family one night and said that to avoid further bloodshed, she was willing to give her virginity and her life. Well, the head of the family took both, and then he slaughtered the princes anyway, all except for one, who escaped to take a terrible revenge. But it is said that ever since that time a curse is laid on this city, that the stones themselves must have blood, or the rivers will dry up and the city be laid to rubble."

"But it seems a very peaceful place now," I objected, thinking of the old men greeting each other in the bars, and women going about doing the shopping, and the tourists beginning to come with their euros and cameras.

"Yes," said Eva, sounding oddly regretful, "But until the death of Hoxha there was still much blood shed in this place, and the stones drank of it. Now all that is done with, Albania is a modern country – but still the city needs blood to live. You have only to ask for his death, and the curse will supply it."

I was shocked and incredulous, but she insisted that the curse was real. "All you have to do," she told me, in a hoarse whisper (for Albanian women often have a rasp in their voice, whether from smoking or some quirk of the language I don't know) "Is to go to Arjuna's house at midnight and wait there for what will come. You won't have to murder anyone, I promise, and by morning Arjuna will be yours, if you wish it, and free. But don't tell Amar what I've said. He'd be very angry that I told you the secret of this curse. He doesn't understand true love."

She said this with a laugh, and I answered her with a hollow laugh of my own, for I had no intention of going back to that ruined house at midnight, on the strength of a bunch of superstitious and bloodthirsty claptrap. If Arjuna wanted to be free of her husband, she only had to divorce him– it was the twenty first century, not the fifteenth!

But somehow, by the following night, I had changed my mind. Whether it was the memory of those heady kisses, or those light-filled eyes, or her serpent-smooth body against mine – I don't know, but against all rationality I decided to go back to that derelict mansion, and try what came of it.

Midnight found me standing in that windswept, dark courtyard, the gargoyles of the gate sneering down at me with their cracked and filthy stone faces. The place stank of cats, and absence. There was no sign of anyone there at all, neither Arjuna, nor her grandmother, nor the man who claimed to be her husband. I picked my way carefully towards the inner room, and switched on my torch, for I'd come prepared – but even the mattresses on the floor had disappeared, together with the black dress hanging in the corner.

I didn't know what to do, so I sat down by the door to, as Eva had told me, to await whatever was to come. Coming there, I'd been frightened and nervous, but now I was there, even though the night was black as a dungeon, I was calm. A strange lethargy took hold of me, and after a while, without realising it, I fell asleep.

When I woke it was even darker, if possible, than before. The moon had disappeared from overhead, and the stars were obscured by a cold haze. I felt, rather than heard or saw, a presence in the room. Now all my fears came rushing back. I thought, what if Eva had tricked me, and sent me here so that Arjuna's husband Antonio could come and murder me? That's what this is all about, not some stupid story about a curse! I was suddenly certain of it, and so I jumped up and scrabbled for my torch, but it had become lost while I was asleep. Searching, I blundered into a wall, and put out my hand to steady myself – and the wall was wet.

Not with water – I could tell by the heavy, sticky feel of it – but with something else. I raised my hand to my face and smelled. It was the rich, sickening tang of new blood, I recognised it instantly. I noticed then that when I lifted my feet from the floor there was a sucking, glutinous pull. Now the smell of blood was all around me, in my nostrils, thick, nauseating. Horrified, I turned towards the courtyard and the outside gate, wiping my hands on my jeans, gasping in my disgust.

And then I stumbled over something, and fell. Reaching out in the darkness, my hand touched rough cloth, but inhabited by something, warm and heavy and very still. To my terror, I realised that it was a body, whether dead or not I didn't know, but it didn't move at all even when I pushed at it in panic, unable to think of anything but my desire to get out of there.

Then – thank God – my foot bumped against something which rattled and bounced on the stone, and reaching down I realised that it was my torch. In relief I turned it on, and saw, in the sudden cold white light, the strangest and most chilling sight.

The tiled floor of the room behind me was moving, with fat, pinkish creatures which seemed to slide and undulate across it, and there were hundreds of them. They were on the walls, too, and among the stones of the courtyard – in fact, I saw more of them emerging from the well as I looked, plopping over the edge like so many great maggots.

As they crawled they seemed to suck and lick at the substance which oozed from the very cracks between the stones – and it *was* blood. More blood than could possibly have come from one person – and yet there was Antonio, slumped on the floor, and he was most definitely dead. He was very pale under his dark tan – it looked odd against the coarse vigorous facial hair – and his skin had a strange withered appearance, as if he had been mummified. He looks, I thought, as if he had been drained.

The creatures were crawling over him, and over my feet, and they were everywhere, growing plumper and redder by the minute. I couldn't help it. I screamed in terror.

And then she was there – Arjuna – and in a moment, as if by magic, they had all disappeared. In the light of my torch she stood there, naked, but more curvaceous than I remembered, and rounder in the face and belly, as if she had eaten a large meal, perhaps, or several. She licked her full, dark-red lips, and smiled at me.

"You came."

She put her pale, suddenly plump arms around my neck, and her salt-tanged lips against mine, and pressed herself against me hungrily. As she kissed me she whispered, "Now you've set me free."

Something came over me, something murderous and lustful and cold, all at once. I carried her to the wall, still soaked with Antonio's blood, and would have made love to her there against the bare stone, drugged with her strange bloated beauty – but just then the darkness was split by a blinding light, and there stood Amar and a half dozen of his friends, with Eva behind them. They all had strong lanterns, and were shining them directly towards us.

Arjuna hissed in my arms. Suddenly the smoothness of her skin felt extremely hot, as if with a fever, but also wet and slippery. She looked into my eyes, hers fierce as a white wolf's, and then it was as if she melted – like some heated liquid, she burned against my skin and then coiled outwards and into the stones of the house, insubstantial as mist. And indeed a faint, pink mist did linger there, coating the stones like an infected sweat...

"I warned you, but you wouldn't listen," Amar said, somewhat smugly, stepping into the courtyard. He prodded Antonio's body. "He is dead. It is not good, for sure, but it is only what happened to the one before, after all. I am glad that it is not your turn, my friend."

I staggered and almost fell to the ground. To tell the truth, the night's events had been too much for me, and I was half faint with shock. He held me up, and guided me out to where a taxi was waiting, owned by a friend of his.

"You had better leave the city of stone, my friend," he said as he helped me inside, "while your luck holds."

"But Arjuna – what happened?" I murmured.

"The Princess and her kind will be looking for a new victim soon," he assured me, his round and cheerful face somewhat grim. "For the stones demand blood. But not yours, I think, not tonight."

I left Gjirokaster, and Albania, the following day, telling my employer I had a sudden illness. I have never been back. Since then, the country has become much more popular among tourists, and my employer's investments extremely profitable. I hear from Amar occasionally, and am pleased to hear that he and his family are prospering.

But I often wonder what happened to Arjuna, and her grandmother, and what really happened that night with Antonio and those horrible slug-like creatures. Did Arjuna find another hapless tourist to snare in her web? Did she suck him dry, as a spider does a fly, in that ancient house under the rock? Or have I been fooled into half-believing the myths of the place, when – it may well turn out - there is some simple, if brutal, explanation.

I will never know – and I don't care to think of it.

It is enough, as Amar said, that it was not me.

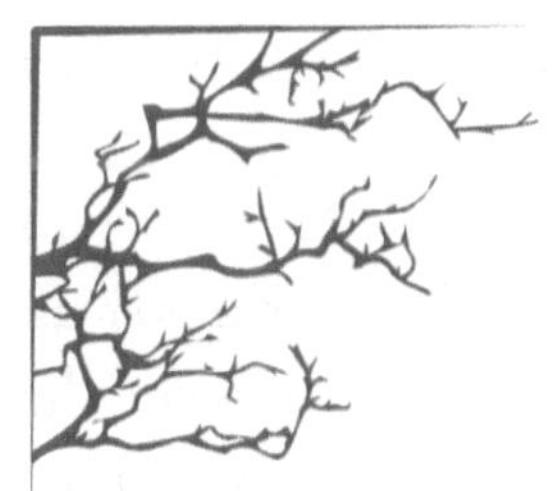

A Celtic tale

It was a wild, cold morning, in a poor stone cottage on the cliffs of Meath, with only the green wastes and the grey sea for midwife. The baby cried as her lungs met the chill sea air, and her mother cradled her under a sheepskin while the shutters shook and the wind keened like a banshee. She called her child Merrow, which means mermaid in the Gaelic tongue, and as she suckled her she muttered a curse to the salt wind.

That very same day, In the High King's seat of Tara, the King's Seer came to him and told him of three omens he had seen. The seer was known as Ciann the Wise, and he had known the King since they were boys together.

"As the sun rose this day," said the Seer, "I saw three swallows swoop on an eagle and blind him, so that he dropped dead from the sky. Later, as the sun was at its zenith, a fisherman came to me with a tale of a fish that sang to him as it was caught, a fair song and sweet, but full of sorrow. And last, as the sun went to its rest and I was returning to your halls, I felt the ground shake under my feet, yet no one felt it but myself."

The High King looked at his Seer long and hard. "We have known each other for twenty five years, Ciann the Wise, and in that time you have seen many true things. But that swallows should blind an eagle, that a fish should sing, and that the earth should shake though no one feel it but you – these things I find hard to believe."

"Difficult to believe they may be, but true they are nevertheless," insisted the Seer.

"Then what is the meaning of these signs, Ciann my friend?" asked the High King in puzzlement.

"This is the meaning I see," said the Seer. "That this day came into the world one who will bring ruin to you and yours, though she is small and weak and you are strong and powerful. She will take from you the sight of your eyes, she will call sorrow from the sea, and she will bring down these walls of earth and wood and all within them."

The King turned pale, and his hands clenched on the arms of the High Seat. "This is ill news you bring me, old friend. But if this be my Fate, it cannot be averted by anything I may do. Is this not so?"

"It is true, a man's Fate cannot be averted, but perhaps yours may yet be. I have seen a vision, and in the vision I saw the Morrigan, Goddess of War and Destiny, she who holds all of our fates in her bloody hands. She spoke to me of three choices by which the path of your Fate may be changed, and all these choices lie in the hand of a girl child. If on her sixteenth birthday the girl wears a red dress, casts a gold ring into the sea, and sings to the grey waters, your doom will be upon you. More than that I cannot tell."

"Where then is this child, who holds my fate in her song?"

"I do not know," said the Seer, "But if you search the land for a girl child born this day, perhaps you will find her."

The High King sent out his messengers across Eire to search for the girl, but they never came to the lonely cottage on the sea cliffs, nor to the two who lived alone there, for mists hid the place from mortal sight. Sixteen years passed, and the girl child grew into a woman. Meanwhile the High King fretted over his fate, while his arm grew feeble and his hair grey as the sea itself.

At last, the sixteenth day since Merrow's birth dawned, and on that day, her mother said to her, "Daughter, today you must wear the red dress I have given you, and place this gold ring upon your finger, for this day we will return to our true home."

"Where is our true home?" asked the girl. "For I thought that it was here, on the green sea coast of Meath."

"Do as I bid you," said her mother sharply, "And do not ask questions."

On that very same day, as it happened, the High King called together all his warriors, and went down to the sea, for ships from the North had come raiding to the land. When he came to the shore and saw the size of the fleet arrayed against him, and the tall warriors crowding forward, their spears like a forest of silver, he turned to his seer and said, "I cannot help but fear, Ciann, that here is my fate come upon me. For there on the cliffs I think I see the Morrigan, her gown red as the battlefield, and she will devour us like a carrion crow before the night falls."

The seer looked up to the cliffs above the bay, and indeed, there was a woman there, dressed in red.

"Perhaps it is the Morrigan," he said slowly, "But that woman is young and fair, and there is an older woman with her. Did not the prophecy speak of a girl in a red dress? I will go now to fetch her, and bring her back here so that you may question her and learn more of this matter." And the High King assented to this, but his heart was full with fear and doubt.

As for the girl, she stood with her mother above the wide grey sea, and as she gazed out, she saw the ships with their golden-haired warriors, their shields numberless as the waves, and she saw also the High King standing by the shore, his warriors beside him, and she said to her mother, "Who are these men in ships, and who are those on the shore?"

"Do not question me, child, but now sing the song that I taught you, fair and sweet and full of sorrow. Sing it to the ocean, that my father Lir may hear you and come to us, and we may go home at last."

But the girl did not heed her. "Mother, who is that King, with white hair and bent back, standing by the shore with his house warriors?"

"Do as I bid you," said her mother.

So Merrow sang to the salt waves the song that her mother had taught her long ago, fair and sweet and full of sorrow, and up from the waves rose Lir, Lord of the Sea, his arms huge as sea serpents, his chest wide as ten ships side by side, hair white as sea foam hanging to his waist. "Who is it that calls to me?" he roared, and the girl's mother cried, "It is I, your daughter, lured sixteen years hence to the green shore for love of a mortal man. But long ago he abandoned me, and now I seek to return to the sea with my child."

Lir fixed his storm-blue eyes upon his daughter and her child. "You are my daughter, and may return when you will. Yet your daughter is half mortal, and like all such children, she must choose her own path. Does she choose to return to the sea of her own free will?"

The mother gave him an angry look. "I am her mother, and have chosen on her behalf. She will do as she is bid."

"Nevertheless," said Lir, "I must hear it from her own mouth. Child, do you wish to live with me as an immortal, under the grey waves, or do you wish to remain mortal, your feet on the solid earth?"

The girl was about to reply, when the Seer hurried up behind them. His breath laboured in his chest, for it was a steep climb, and he was old.

"Do not choose until you know the nature of your choice," he told her. "Before you speak, ask your mother the reason why she bade you wear a red dress on this day, and to place a gold ring on your finger?"

The mother would have refused to answer, but Lir was curious, and commanded her.

"She wears a red dress," she said reluctantly, "So that the Morrigan may recognize her, and fulfil my curse upon the man who fathered her. The gold ring was given to me by the High King of Tara in token of his love, but he betrayed me, and when his daughter shall cast that ring into the sea, the Morrigan has promised me that my curse will be fulfilled. The High King's warriors will be vanquished, his high seat of Tara shall be burned to the ground, and he himself will be blinded and thrown into the deep waters."

"Then let my granddaughter choose," said Lir, "If she chooses to cast the ring into the sea, your curse shall be fulfilled. And if not, the High King will have victory today, and die in his bed. I warn you, however, daughter, that a bargain made with the Morrigan is not easily put aside."

The mother turned to her daughter, and commanded her to cast the golden ring, but the girl shook her head. "I do not wish to do this thing, mother, and bring about the deaths of many men, among them my own father."

"Do as you are bid," said her mother. "Your father promised me marriage, and that I would sit beside him in his Great Hall as Queen of all Eire, but he left me for another woman before you were born. I have cursed him, and he must die."

And still Merrow hesitated. "I cannot kill my own father, and your curse is none of mine."

And then her mother said to her, "If you do not do this, daughter, you will surely die in his place. For a bargain is a bargain, and the Morrigan must have blood this day. If not theirs," and she pointed to the warriors waiting upon the shore, "then yours."

Lir, meanwhile, had grown impatient. "Come to me, or stay where you are, I care not, but make up your mind. The Morrigan waits on no woman, nor I neither."

Then the Seer, who was quick of wit despite his age, said, "If the Morrigan must have blood this day, why should she not take it from the north men in their dragon ships, and not from this innocent girl?" He turned to the girl. "Why not leave here, and come with me? Your father will be glad indeed to find he has a daughter, and as a princess of Tara, you will be well cared for and greatly beloved."

"Whether she casts the ring or not, victory comes to the strongest," Lir pointed out, "and your King is weak and outnumbered, while his enemy is brave and fierce."

"But," said the girl, who had seen the direction of the Seer's thoughts, "could not you, who are Lord of the salt sea, raise up the wind and the waves against these men in their strange ships, and drive them from shore, to sink and drown in your green depths?"

"I could," Lir said, "But why should I?"

"Because you are my mother's father."

"I have many daughters, and my grandchildren are as numerous as the fishes."

"Because the High King my father will give you gifts of gold and silver, and all the treasure that you desire, in return for his life and his throne."

"What use have I of gold and silver, who have the treasures of a thousand wrecks to gild my halls?"

In desperation the girl said, "Then what can I give you to avert my father's fate?"

Lir laughed. "Life must have death, and the Morrigan must be paid, for even I am subject to her weavings. Take off your red dress, leave your gold ring upon the shore, and cast yourself naked from these cliffs, and I will ensure your father's victory and the ruination of his enemies."

"No!" cried the mother, "You must not do this!"

Swiftly then the girl tore the red dress from her body, tossed the gold ring to the Seer, and naked she flung herself from the cliffs to the sea far below. And the mother wailed and tore at her hair, and the Morrigan laughed her dreadful laugh as she rode through the dark clouds above. Lir spoke words of command, and the wind rose high and howling, and drove the northmen's ships away from the shore, and many of the warriors sank with their weapons and their treasure to augment the hoard of Lir beneath the waves.

Merrow would have drowned with them, but her mother's father caught the girl in his watery grasp, and returned her to the shore, where her father the High King stood waiting. His heart rejoiced at the sight of her, for he had not known he had a daughter. Her mother had hidden it from him these long years in anger, since he had broken his promise to her and lain with another woman. The High King lived, and ruled another score of years to die in his bed, far from the Fate foretold. But a bargain is a bargain, and a curse must be honoured. So Merrow's mother was snatched up by the Morrigan in her arms of flame, as she stood there on the cliffs, and borne away upon the wind, never to see her own true home again.

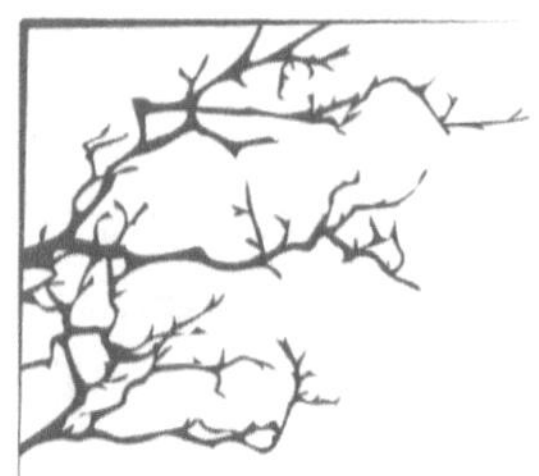

The Plague

They say that in the weeks before the Great Plague, ships were seen gliding on the sea, calm flowing forth from under their keels like the spreading dark. Those who saw them pass by tell a tale of shadow men crowding the smooth decks, clawed hands and seared skin and eyes like the cinders of a blasted city. Watching from the shore, far as they were, they smelled the stench of decay on a ghost wind, and soon after fell into a sleep, and then into grey death.

When the rulers were told of these wonders, they sent their own ships to find and destroy the demon vessels, but these were lost in a strange, foul mist that crept up from the west, and never seen again. So the rulers ordered the people to move inland, away from the demons who roamed the wide waters.

It was not long before death caught up with them. It moved through the rivers and the streams, swimming serpent-like against tide and current. It leaked into the dewdrops as they formed on the spring green grass, and into the rain as it kissed each roof and slab. It caressed the soft curls of babies as they lay in their mothers' arms and the wispy remnants on the heads of the old. It rode in on a breath and out on a sigh, and everywhere there was water, there was sickness.

So the rulers bade their servants lock the gates, and the people went inside their houses and shut their doors, and those who could drank wine, and those who could not drank nothing, and died of their thirst. At last even the wine was gone, and the rulers turned to each other and said, how shall we preserve ourselves?

Then the man said to the woman, the only wine that remains is that which runs in the veins of our children. It is a good vintage, for we made it ourselves. The woman refused, saying, I would rather join the numberless dead than drink that vintage, no matter how rare and red. The man, maddened by his thirst and his desire to live, killed both the woman and their children, and sated himself, and lived. In time, he looked over his walls to find that the Plague had ended.

So he unlocked the great gates and walked out into the silent world, where only the bones muttered against one another in the dry breeze. The rivers and streams had withered, the sea was a plain of salt, and the rain a fearful memory. Then he wept; his tears were red as wine and blood, and hissed as they fell on the scorched ground.

Or so they say, for that was long ago, and far away, and now they are all dead who knew the truth of it.

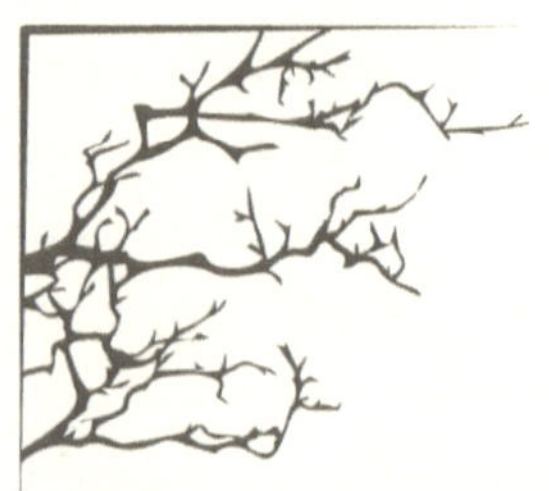

The Outsider

This isn't a social visit.

It's a delegation. With their storm cloud beards and hats crushed over bald spots, they arrive at her door like an advance guard, like Mr Death from the village, multiplied. Mick and Bill O'Keefe from down by the river flats – one fat and one lean, as if they graze on different pasture. Jock the mechanic with his blistered guitar fingers and dreadlocks. Rob the slasher (and fencer and road roller and conqueror of African love grass and what have you) with his jeans all tight like he's from Texas and not some boggy Gippsland valley.

Their wives don't like her. "I won't cross that threshold," she's heard one of them say, in the General Store, and "Velvet curtains. What's she going for then, the bordello look?" Country women with chainsaws and egg beaters, stout and grizzled. They have no use for art.

"Boots off if you don't mind, gentlemen." But they're already scuffing off their Blundstones, great slops of paddock rich mud slapping the concrete porch, and shaking the rain from their jackets. Deliberately they avoid looking at her. She's too much for them, with her silk pyjama pants and Moroccan tunic and hair as red as earth.

She ushers them in from the wet. Past the fin de siècle mirrors and the tasselled floor lamps and the inlaid occasional tables she picked up from a deceased estate in Melbourne. Past the paintings of Indian goddesses and mermaids. Into the old bistro. The men don't know where to put their big gnarled hands; it feels wrong to be standing here in their socks, where the old pool table used to be. "Remember old Sally?" one of them mutters under his breath, "He'd be rolling."

"Do sit down, gentlemen."

They sit, spreading their knees modestly.

"It's about the open mic night."

"Oh yes..."

"We always used to hold it here, back when Bunty ran the place. So we were wondering..."

"Well Mick," she says, "I'm very keen to encourage local talent."

Only that's not the sort of talent she had in mind when she bought the place, the old pub with its rotten floorboards and leaking tin roof and back garden full of beer cans and rotted fag ends. She saw past it and through it and around it; she recognised it as a *setting*. Like a ring lying in the dirt, missing its stone.

You don't find such a setting, and lovingly shape and polish the jewel that will sit in it, and slide it on to your finger - and then finish the look off with cow-stained jeans and blue singlets. You don't create a thing of beauty and then fill it with rednecks who think they're Bob Seeger or Slim Dusty, farmers whose idea of poetry is there's a redback on the toilet seat and Banjo Patterson on a milk crate, you don't.

"That's good to hear," says Mick – the fat one, with a nose upturned as the pigs he raises and his face pitted with skin cancer scars - and he's about to go on, with the case they've obviously nutted out between them in the kitchens of conspiracy, but Maeve gets in first.

"But of course we have bookings right through this month and then you know how busy it gets in January..."

"You got gigs booked?"

"Not exactly..." She's tried to get musicians from as far afield as Melbourne, people she knows from the scene, but first Covid, then the rain. "Guests. At the B&B. And there's a yoga workshop on next weekend, and, you know how it is."

"Yoga eh." Rob the slasher stretches out his cowboy-lean legs as if he's claiming squatting rights. "Maybe they'd like a bit of music. Adds to the ambi-ence." He pronounces it like Beyonce.

"I'm afraid not." They come – when they come – to enjoy elegant candlelit dinners in front of the restored open fireplace, and the rising of the moon over the mountains. They don't come now, mind you, when the landscape is soggy and the skies liquid. There's no need to say that, though.

"But Bunty always used to have the music, first Saturday of the month," Jock objects. Itching, no doubt, to get up there and deafen them all.

"And darts on Fridays," adds Mick's brother Bill. The lean one. Eighty-five if he's a day and still patrolling the ancestral acreage with his dog and tractor – she's seen him at it as she drives past to lunch in town. They keel over in the mud, these people; they don't give up.

It's difficult. They all think the place is theirs, they all want to put it back the way it was. That's gone, she wants to tell them, and it wasn't as good as you think, anyway. Drunken out-of-towners throwing their bottles on the road. The bar smelling of hay, red-faced dairy baronets roaring at each other in the front garden at midnight. She wants a salon. Artists, writers, people who will bring a little colour and zest to this yawning, sheep-drunk valley. They live like peasants huddled under the grandeur and wonder of their surroundings; they scoff at beauty.

So no, there will be no screeching of harmonicas and crooning of bush ditties in the front bar, and she is considering how to put this in a way that's firm yet diplomatic, when the front door slams – she winces, because the stained glass cost a bundle – and it's the Icelander.

He's not *from* Iceland, that's just how she thinks of him. He must be easily six foot five and built like a church wall; his drizabone swirls about him as if blown by an invisible breeze, the same kind that lifts the hair of Scandinavian models on mountain sides. He is a god.

"Maeve!" he calls out, in some European accent she hasn't managed to pin down (but it's not Icelandic, he told her so. Guess, he said). "Maeve, where are you hiding?"

The old men grin. They don't like Maeve, and they don't like anyone, by extension, who likes Maeve, but they like the Icelander. He is a bloke's bloke, a subduer of noxious weeds and feral animals, a wielder of fire hoses, a dependable and yet self-sufficient neighbour. Their wives like him even better; they compliment him on his pumpkins and think of him, secretly, in their grizzled dreams. Or so Maeve guesses.

"Oh, Bjorn!" (His name isn't really Bjorn. It's Karl. "But Bjorn suits you!" she has said, gaily. So Bjorn it is.) "We were just discussing music nights, and I was just explaining..."

"The river's rising," he says to the men. Ignoring her.

In moments they're on their feet, tipping themselves towards her, shuffling towards the door in their woolly black socks. It's a relief, to be honest. Of course, if they don't go now, they'll be cut off. The river is a temperamental thing, given to boiling over its causeways in a storm, subsiding like a spoilt kid once the rain lets up. More than once they've had to stay in town, here. At Bunty's, when he ruled the pub. Now, Maeve does, and she would rather not.

"Aren't you going too?" she coos at him, after the delegation has departed, unsatisfied. Thank the rain for that. On and on it goes, all summer, but she hasn't minded. One can live – almost – on art alone. She has been painting landscapes in shades of green and grey.

The Icelander is planted in the carpet like Megatron. "You should leave, also. While the road is open."

"Oh, I'll be fine here, it's not going to be a problem." Flattered that he cares, though.

"Well," he says (only, with his accent, it's more of a 'vell'. Charming.) "It is not looking good. Don't say I didn't warn you."

She would like him to insist a little more, over a cup of something. But he just pulls his cloak – his drizabone, but it has the look of a cloak – around him and flicks his grey ponytail, as coarse and virile as a stallion, and before she can say, "Wait a minute, Bjorn, can I offer you a..." he's back in his old Range Rover with the red kelpie sticking its nose out the window and he's gone and she's alone again, with the art.

When she rises the next morning in her cream silk komono, bought in Kyoto, the genuine article, the road out is cut in both directions. She wades across to the General Store in her wellies – not that there's flooding, not here, but the water's above ankle height and ugg boots just won't do – to buy milk and butter. There's no one behind the counter.

"Yoo hoo!"

"You still here, Maeve?" Josephine pops her head in from the back. Mick's niece – they're all related, these farm-grown families whose grandfathers drove bullock ploughs across indigenous hunting grounds, but she's always been friendly, Josephine. She even put her name down for the yoga workshop, "Though with the rain, Maeve, I'm not sure..."

"We're just packing up," she says now, cheerily. "Have you got somewhere to go?"

"Oh darling, it's sweet of you to ask, but I'll be fine."

"Are you sure? They're saying we'll get two hundred mill overnight..."

"I'll manage. I've got plenty of Long Life." Maeve has looked into the flood situation. You don't buy green without expecting wet, and you don't begin a business without checking. The pub sits high; in the old days, so Josephine told her, men used to roll down from the porch to the road, sozzled, to be slung into the back of their wives' Ford utes and hauled back home over the boiling causeways.

But Josephine has already disappeared to her boxes. Maeve can hear the kids squealing as they help, or get in the way. Sloshing back across the road, she lifts her umbrella to take in the mountains, the scenic scallop to this emerald bowl of a place. But there are no mountains, today; the wall of cloud has swallowed them. How do you represent a world of glass and mist?

By nightfall the town is ghostly, barely in existence. Maeve puts candles in her windows; she feels as if she, alone, is guarding the light of the world. The road is a low roar, the General Store a theory. Darkness rushes past her porch. Is she the only person still here in the village? It feels like it. Can you paint rain in the night? Van Gogh might have tried. Already the floorboards, replaced entirely a year ago, feel wet-cold under her bare feet. And what of the antique sofas? The grand piano? At least, she thinks, I could sit on top of it, if it comes to it – that thing wouldn't move if Moses commanded.

Morning, and now she *could* paint, but a flood isn't a thing of beauty. Across the road brown mire laps at the check-curtain windows of the General Store. Josephine and her husband Matt will be scraping noxious mud from their chocolate box shop for months, if there's anything left of it, afterwards. Mick and Bill will be herding their flocks into the hills, crouching under jolly tarps while their grizzled wives make damper, coping. Their sort complain, but don't go under. They hold their lives inside themselves; when disaster strikes, the essentials are kept dry, waiting. She, on the other hand, has put her soul into the doors, the windows, the soft furnishings. Even now, as she watches, treacle fingers of wet come questing under the French doors.

And an engine thrusts to a halt beyond the bay window, and someone shouts, "Maeve!" and it's the Icelander. Like a Viking he is, standing in the prow of his tinnie, roped up to a telephone pole, with his cloak flapping about him and his ponytail whipping and his eyes the blue of Caracao liqueur in a cut glass goblet. She opens the door to him and to the whole world which comes puddling in over her polished wood floor, as if a thousand Micks and Bills and Bobs had come in out of the rain with their boots still on and their raincoats dripping.

"Get in," he commands. Her shy and lonely heart flutters, because to be honest she has been lonely, as the hated often are, even while her soul turns back to the pub, still bound by the grand piano and the paintings and the *trouble* she went to. He nods towards the shrouded hills. "You can stay at mine."

"I can't just leave."

"You want to swim?"

The bar is awash; the water is the colour of beer.

"Bjorn, I can't! What will happen to it all?"

"My name isn't Bjorn," he says with a trace of Germanic irritation, "I told you. And we will help. We will all help one another."

Tell that to the wives, she thinks. Looks back at the velvet drapes flirting with the flood.

"They won't."

His hair is alight with seed pearls of rain. "You will have to put in a pool table, perhaps. And let them have their music."

She fetches a suitcase. A delegation can be refused – even the Icelander can be wheedled, perhaps, with the cream silk kimono and the best Borneo beans. But the land, it seems, has the last word.

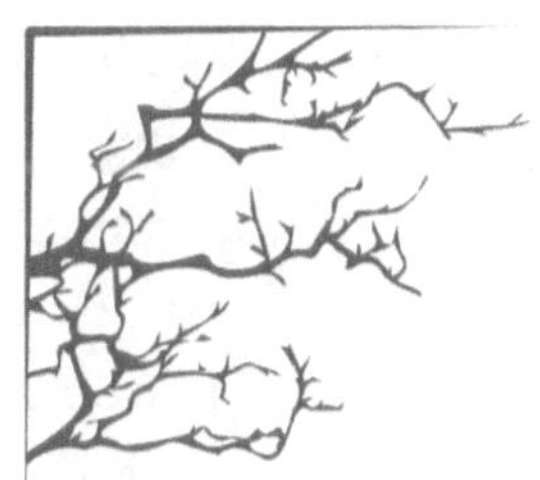

Goddess

My name is Artemis. I am tall, and strong, and ugly as a sow in heat, they tell me.

When I was born to my mother Hera, I'm told she took one look at me and said, "Take her out and put her in the barn with the brutes." I didn't mind, I dare say, I've always had an affinity with animals. For what are we but animals, some of us with a little more wit and most of us with a lot more greed?

I was big even then for a goddess, and I didn't stay a baby for long. I crawled amongst the horses and cows, and got up on their backs and nestled my face into their warm harsh fur. I clambered out into the fields and woods and stuck my head down burrows, sniffing at their occupants. And they sniffed right back at me, and sometimes snarled and clawed at my face. I didn't care, I was immortal and couldn't be harmed by such as they. So I poked and prodded and snarled back, and eventually they accepted me as just another animal, a cub who didn't know what she was doing but was harmless enough.

I was happy in the woods, and would have been happy in the barn, but even a child goddess must go home sometime. When I came back to my mother's palace, my hair matted with the sweat of the day, my face caked in dirt and my body covered with scratches, my mother hissed at me with disgust and told my nursemaid to take me away and feed me in the servants quarters, for I was not fit for a god's table.

Much I cared – for even then I did not like my mother. She was a woman who cared for nothing but power, and since my father Zeus, as Lord of the gods, possessed most of it, she was perpetually unhappy. She would order the servants, setting them difficult and wearying tasks, insisting that everything be done in a particular manner and in a particular time. Every day she would inspect the household minutely to see that all had been done as she commanded. Inevitably, she would find that it had not, and then she would rage and shout and insist that it be done all over again, secretly pleased by their mistakes. She would redecorate the palace two or three times a week, dissatisfied with the placement of mirrors or the colour of a ceiling – she would do it on a whim, having only to think of what she desired, and then prowl about looking for anything that did not fit. In short, she was chronically frustrated.

It was easy to be ugly; I did not mind. An ugly girl is spared the trouble of arranging her hair in cumbersome curls or fussing over her dress or trotting about in uncomfortable shoes. As I grew, I chose my weapons, as all the gods do – but not the goddesses. I have never seen why it should be so. Except that the goddesses, for the most part, prefer to play games amongst themselves, to rival each other in love, raise their godlings, and – of course – bully mortals. For an immortal strength is not an accident of birth, as it is for a mortal; it is an attribute of power and of mind. Any goddess could choose to have muscles like my own, iron banded legs, sinews of steel, a chest as broad as a bear and a skull as thick. But she wants to be admired, generally speaking, and so does not. Males, even among the gods, do not take their rivals to bed.

Womanhood came to me, as it does to the gods, quickly and without the blood and mess, spots and stormy tempers that accompany it in mortals. I simply woke one morning, and turned to my shield (for I had no mirror) to see that I had grown breasts and hips and hair in places where it was not before. I examined myself closely, decided that it would do, and threw on a tunic to go out to the hunt.

I should explain that by this time I was not a friend to all animals as I had been before. The gods do not need to eat meat – they do not need to eat at all – but long ago they caught the habit from mortals and got the taste for blood and burnt flesh. They also caught the habit of hunting, and that was not so foreign to them, for we have always enjoyed killing, even if it is just each other. What would you? Eternity is a tedious thing, and we must needs enliven it somehow. Since the great War, particularly, gods have turned to hunting (both humans and other animals) and to sports and games of all kinds. Including, as you know, the Great Game.

On this morning, I went out to hunt in the forest of Arcadia, a wild place on earth where one might still sometimes find strange beasts such as unicorns and centaurs, although for the most part I hunted wild boar or deer. I took with me my great iron spear, my bow and a quiver of arrows, and a brace of wolf pups I had trained to help track and hold.

Soon enough the wolves picked up a trail, and we went running together through the pathless forest, the dogs in a flurry with their noses to the ground, I picking my way behind over the bracken and bog. It is hard to explain what a joy it is to have your feet meet the earth, bare and unprotected, so that you can feel all the textures of it – boggy, gravelled, warm leaf litter, cold stone, even prickles and thorns – meet your bare skin at each falling step. I admit, there is something about the human world that I love, beautiful as Olympos is. I love that you cannot easily change it. Anything in Olympos is as you please; my mother changes her rooms as often as she wants, with just a thought and a wish. Our world is woven from thought, and I think that if we all died, it would die with us.

Not the mortal world. If all humans were to perish tomorrow, the world would survive, and be glad of it. Humans are a pestilence, that is the truth of it, like a swarm of mites on a peach tree. But nature, in the mortal world, meets you as an equal. When you run, the sweat runs off you, whether you will or no. At night, the air is cold on your skin. When you leap into a lake, you sink or you swim, but you cannot walk across it. Unless you are a god, of course, and then you can do many things. But I choose not to; it is much more fun that way.

So, we were running through the forest, the leaves and twigs scratching my arms as I brushed past them, when the wolves began to bay. The boar was close; they smelled its run. I came up behind them, panting, and signalled to them that they should circle around behind the beast and drive it towards me. They were well trained animals, and understood me almost as well as if we could speak; indeed, we did speak, mind to mind.

The wolves obeyed. Three went one way, three another, and I waited. Soon there was a great noise of crashing branches and undergrowth trampled underfoot, and the boar came rushing out, red eyed and furious. I did not blame it; I would have been furious too, in its situation. I readied my spear, its haft resting against the ground between my feet, and the boar came charging at me, its head lowered. I was not in the least afraid, of course. I could have incinerated the animal with a glance, but that would have been no sport. I braced myself, and smelled its rank smell. No ranker than my own, if the truth be told.

I felt the animal surge onto my spear, its flesh ramming up into the steel. Still on it came. I could not help but admire its courage. Its blood spurted out at me, covering me in gouts of thick scarlet. I looked into its tiny eyes, and saw there such a determination to live and conquer that I found myself in sympathy with the animal. If it had been born with power such as mine, who knows where it would be – probably in Ares' seat at the high table in Olympos. And I would rather see the boar sitting there than Ares, the fat bearded prick.

The boar had collapsed to the ground in its last agonies, its legs still kicking at the dirt and its mouth champing. I braced my foot against it and pulled out the spear, releasing yet more blood. The grass was slippery with it, the gore squelching up between my bare toes. I knelt down and scratched the animal behind its ears, as if it could still feel my affection. I thought, perhaps I will resurrect you. Let you live to fight again, to breed and live. You and I are alike – we are both strong and fierce, and we are both called pigs.

But I was hot and filthy. There was a stream nearby, that fell into a pool, deep and bordered by large rocks. It was a still and lovely place, and I had often dived in on other occasions and felt the cold water envelop my limbs and shock my tired muscles into renewed vitality.

I bid the wolves guard the carcass, and then I walked the short distance to my bathing pool. I was standing at the part of the stream that ran just above the pool, over which a small waterfall glittered and bounced, and had a good view of what was below me. And there I stopped, in shock and rage. There was a man on the rocks below, and he was washing his hands and his face. In *my* pool!

I reached for the bow that hung on my back. My immediate thought was to rid me of this human nuisance –and then I had a second thought, and paused. This forest was forbidden to mortals; my priests had told them so, in no uncertain terms. Whoever was wandering here, then, was either ignorant, or insolent. He was unaware of the law, or he *was* aware of it, and had breached it for some reason that seemed good to him. If unaware – well, it so happened that I was in a merciful mood, and might allow him to escape with nothing more than a fright. I was an apparition to frighten anyone. I was covered in blood and sweat, my eyes glowed white as molten steel and I stood over eight feet tall, which is tall for a goddess, never mind a mortal woman.

But if he had reason... then what could it be? Did he think to beard the goddess in her lair and ask a gift or offer up some pathetic prayer for personal favour? I watched him as he shook droplets of water from his curly dark hair, and looked up – not to the top of the fall, where I stood, but blankly into the middle distance, as if he did not quite know what to do next.

It is not the first time that one of my kind has fallen in love with a mortal, or in lust. But since I was old enough to understand it, I have always despised such things as beneath me. It was all very well for

Aphrodite to go sniffing about on earth for men to toy with, for Athena to bat her eyes at mortals and expect fatuous poetry in return – but not for me. Now, suddenly, I understood them. This boy was beautiful. His eyes were the deep cloudy green of the pool itself, his lips were fringed by the barest hint of a moustache, less than my own. He was bare to the waist, his chest was adorned with a light fuzz, and his shoulders were smooth and shapely.

Ah, but beauty is not the point, I reminded myself, thinking of Aphrodite and her witless loveliness. He is still a trespasser, and his life is forfeit, as soon as I discover what brought him here. I was about to make myself known to him – and doubtless frighten the life out of him – when evidently something funny must have crossed his mind, for he smiled. And that was the arrow that felled me. I had never seen such an artless, sunny and mischievous smile. We gods are not known for our sense of humour, and when we laugh, it is usually out of malice. But this boy – you could see the laughter in the creases beneath his river green eyes and in the deep dimples at the corners of his mouth. I was enraptured at once. And then his face fell, and became blank once more. He stood up, as if to go.

I was charmed. So instead of bellowing out in my most fearsome roar, I opened my mouth to speak to him softly – and then I caught sight of my reflection in the stream and thought better of it. If the poor boy saw me like this, he'd probably have a heart attack, even if I whispered in the most dulcet of tones.

In a moment I was light and lithe, with honey gold hair and eyes of soft brown and skin smooth as milk, and stepping down towards him like a gazelle to a waterhole. You, mortal, may wonder why I was not *always* like this, if I could change my appearance with just a thought. Wouldn't every woman choose to be pretty instead of ugly, if she only could? But you see, an individual, mortal or immortal, is a whole thing, mind and body together, and even a goddess must be what she truly is.

Finally he looked up at me, when my white feet rustled in the fallen leaves, and his ripe mouth fell open to show teeth perfect as a child's.

"I am Artemis, lady of the forest? Why do you enter my domain?" I said softly, so as not to alarm him.

He cleared his throat, a discreet, adorable sound.

"Forgive me, goddess. I did not come here of my own will. I would never, that is, never willingly, disturb your sanctuary, but I..."

"Do not be afraid, mortal." This is the way I imagined then that goddesses should speak to mortals – measured, condescending. "Then if not your will, whose?"

His long eyelids drooped. "My brother cast me out from our father's house, and hunted me with men and dogs. There was nowhere to go but the forest, but once I came among the trees, I could not get out again. It was as if – as if the trees had a purpose, to lead me astray and confine me, otherwise I would not have dared to go further in. I know it is forbidden."

I was curious, even more now. It sometimes seems to me that mortals and gods are very alike in some ways. We goddesses do not bear our siblings much affection either. "Why did your brother cast you out? Was it some act of impiety, some fault of your own?"

I could imagine this boy taking part in some mischief, but not a serious crime, murder or incest or anything like that.

"He was jealous," the boy said simply, his eyes sliding away awkwardly. "My father preferred me. I never asked for it. But he is away on business, and so my brother took the opportunity to be rid of me. He will say that I ran away, or got myself killed on some escapade."

Again, it was not so very different from Olympos. Mortals are always conspiring against one another; it passes the time. Still, I found myself becoming angry with this brother of his. Perhaps I might stop by his house one day and with a flick of my finger have him dead of the plague, or a stone fall upon his head.

"How wicked!" I said gently, and floated to his side. I put my hand on his shoulder. "Let me comfort you."

Now, you will probably think this very forward for a newly fledged goddess, her womanly breasts not a day old on her chest, and her loins unblooded. But with my breasts and my body hair had come urges; I had not been aware of them until this moment, but now they heated within me like a clay pot in a kiln. I remembered the gossip I'd heard from Athena and Aphrodite and the fertility goddesses sitting about with their weaving, about mortal sex, and men's needs, and how to entice a man's body before you bind his soul in bands of iron. So I shrugged off my tunic and stood before him, watching to see his reaction.

It was surprise. He stepped back, putting his hands behind him as if he was afraid to touch me, and his eyes widened. Didn't he want me? I was embarrassed now, and felt myself blushing.

"But you're – so far above me, most blessed Artemis. I should not be seeing..."

Are you kidding? I looked back at him, and my first thought, I admit, was to stretch out my hand, push him down onto the mossy rock and have my way with him, virgin goddess or no. But his look of genuine bewilderment gave me pause.

"Do you not... find me attractive?" I fluttered my eyelashes as Aphrodite would have. It felt distasteful. Still, the mortal seemed to like it, despite himself; his eyes kept flickering to my breasts and my hips, and then, guiltily, back up to my divine face. I came closer, and put my arms about his neck, my body brushing against his.

He was a man, as the fertility goddesses had said. He rose against my bare belly, tenting his drawstring trousers. I was sick of playing modest. I reached for the drawstring and the trousers fell to the earth. "Come then," I said, trying to keep the peremptory tone out of my voice, "make love to me, mortal, for I desire you."

We went to a soft place under the trees, where the autumn leaves fell deep, and he fucked me. It was wonderful. Immortals have many ways to fuck, and mortals only one, but it is a good one. The thing that gave me the most pleasure, though, was to look down at his face afterwards, and see that warm, lazy, mischievous mortal smile spreading across his sweet face, as he drew me down and kissed me on the lips.

"I am not sorry, now, that my brother hunted me into the forest." His face clouded. "Unless you meet to kill me now, goddess. Now that you have taken what you wanted."

"What do you take me for?" I said, and then thought, he is right. There are plenty of gods, and goddesses, who would take a mortal for lust and then put an end to him, on a whim. My sister Athena would do it.

But as we lay there, I wondered what I was going to do with him. By the sounds of it, his life was forfeit to his brother if he went home. But the forest was not a place designed for a mortal to live, and besides, I still did not like the idea of someone – even someone as handsome as this boy – roaming my personal hunting grounds.

"Are you fond of your brother?" I asked, fondling his hair, so glossy and chestnut dark.

He turned his face towards me, serious. "No. I hate him. It was not my fault that my father preferred me, and yet he would have murdered me for it."

"So if something were to happen to him, you would not be distressed?"

"No, goddess, I would not be distressed. But - "

"Go home," I said, "when you arrive, you will find that your brother has met with an unfortunate accident. Bury him with honour, and say nothing of this meeting. All I demand is that once a week, on this day, you return to the forest and meet me here, at sunset. Agreed?"

I have come to the conclusion, since, that perhaps my brisk instructions were not overly romantic. I should have talked of love, and my desire for him, and pleaded for him to visit me rather than commanded it. But I was never good at manipulating the emotions of humans or gods; I knew what I wanted, I said what I wanted, and they could agree or refuse, as they wished. I am not a subtle goddess.

He looked at me with a wary softness, and smiled again so that it almost melted my heart.

"I will live only for that day that we meet, goddess," he said, and got up, and drew on his trousers once more.

We said farewell, and when he arrived home his brother had indeed died – an ox had kicked him in the skull as he passed behind its stall, and stove in his brain. My boy – whose name was Actaeon – became the heir and in a few months inherited his father's lands and riches. His father had died in a shipwreck, it was none of my doing. Just so you know.

Each week we met and made love, and I grew more and more enthralled. It was not just his smile, or his full, curving lips like the prow of a boat; there was a charm about him that made you want to draw close and warm your hands, made even me – a goddess – long for his interest and approval. In Olympos, no one had approved of me. I was too ugly and boisterous for my mother, my male cousins found me boring and the other goddesses said that I stank. So I suppose I was ripe for some mortal to make me feel as if I mattered for a moment.

Still, after we had known each other for a few months, something niggled at me. Each time we met, as with the first time, I transformed myself into a shape that I despised, for Actaeon's benefit. I dressed myself in soft curves, made my face round and regular, my body hairless, weak and smooth. I lowered my voice and pretended, as far as I was able, to be shy and maidenly. They said – those wily goddesses who knew – that that was what men liked, and who was I to disagree.

But to me, it felt wrong. When Actaeon looked on me, as we were making love, he wasn't seeing *me*, he was seeing some simpering goddess who was nothing like me. I found myself wondering, more and more often, what he would say if he saw the real Artemis. Would he shrink back in disgust? Would he blink, and pretend to feel just the same, but I would see in his eyes and in his cock that he no longer had desire for me?

Well, it ate at me, and so one day, when we were reclining by the pool that we had made our own, I stroked his cheek and whispered,

"Actaeon, my darling, most handsome of men – is your love for my beauty alone, or would you still desire me if I were tall and plain and strong, like a butcher's wench?"

You will say it was a stupid question – for one should never ask questions of a man unless one wishes to know the true answer – and you would be right. But Actaeon looked startled and thoughtful. Then he kissed me, and said,

"Sweetheart, my goddess, beauty captivates a man, but character keeps him. Were you to change into the Medusa herself, you could not be less than beautiful to me."

And this, to be honest, was a very stupid thing for a mortal to say. For I was a goddess, and for all he knew might change myself into the Medusa in a fraction of second, and turned him to stone where he lay.

"Then I will be honest with you, my love. My true being is not as you see me now, nor is it like to the Medusa. Would you like to see me as I really am?"

He looked a little frightened, at that, and well he might. But he put a brave face on it, having committed himself already, and said, "Of course I would. I long for it. As long," he added, "as you do not intend to appear as the sun and scorch me into a smear of charcoal where I lie."

I laughed at this – it was a joke – and he laughed too. "No, nothing like that," I reassured him, and then I stood up, feeling naked and shy, and I let him see me.

After I had changed, I was afraid to look at him, for fear of his response. I lowered my eyes – not something I am in the habit of doing, for I am not naturally modest – and turned away, waiting for his comment. In a moment of the rustle of the leaves, and felt his hand reaching up to my shoulder, gently resting there. I looked down at him, for I was now much taller, and wider too.

"You are more beautiful even than you were before," he said, and the hand that had been on my shoulder dropped to cup my breast. He kissed it, and I rested my chin in his curls. I was filled with relieved happiness. He lifted his face to mine and I could not find in it any trace of revulsion, but he did look serious for once, and thoughtful. "To tell the truth, I have been wondering for a while whether you have been hiding something from me. When I look into your face, it is like looking into a mist, lovely as it is. Now your... outside seeming and your soul match. I prefer it."

Now, there is something that mortals do not know about gods. We do not have souls. But I let it pass, because I understood what he was trying to say. We sat for a long time by the pool, just holding hands, his lean and small boned, mine larger, brown and strong as a vice. For the first time with him, I felt completely at peace.

The next day, as I was prancing about my mother's palace grounds, filled with unreasoning happiness, my half sister Aphrodite crossed my path. As usual, she was dressed in some clinging silken thing, with her golden hair rippling down her back and her arms hung about with jangling bracelets of silver and gold. If Aphrodite ever attempted to hunt, the beasts would hear her coming a mile away, and the birds see her flashing like a cat's collar.

"What are you so pleased about, Artemis?" she trilled, looking me up and down as if I was a cow that had got out of the pen. "Have your eyebrows grown another inch thicker? Or is it your moustache?"

"I am in love, with a man that loves me," I boasted, wanting to share my pleasure. Aphrodite could prink and primp and act the idiot (not that she had to act, for she truly was an idiot) to ensnare the men, but I had no need. For I had a man who loved me just as I was, warts and all, and wasn't that better than all her silly artifice?

"Oh! Is that so? Are you talking of one of Zeus's bulls, perhaps, or perhaps some peasant too blind with age to see what he is sticking his dick into?"

Her words rolled off me like pebbles from a glacier. I was too full of self-love to care what she said. But a few days later I was attending – perforce – one of the feasts my father Zeus throws periodically for the greater glory of Olympos and himself, and Aphrodite came to me at table. She was Zeus's favourite child, and wherever she went eyes followed her beauty; well she knew it and made the most of it.

"Sister Artemis," she said in her high, whiny voice, "I was so pleased to hear that you had finally got yourself a lover, that I just had to go and see him for myself. I was ever so impressed. Such a fine, handsome boy, who would have thought it!"

I stared at her. She went to see Actaeon? Her eyes glittered with mischief, but I was frozen in my seat. My mother Hera looked down at us.

"What are you talking to Artemis about, Aphrodite? Some gossip that we all should hear? Do tell!"

"Oh, it's nothing, but Artemis has found herself a man. A sweet young thing, well shaped and well mannered. We had quite the conversation, actually."

"And what did you talk about?" I forced myself to say. I was sure, looking at the spite in her baby blue eyes, that she had tried to seduce him. And I was not at all sure that she had failed. I thought, I will catch her one night when she is alone, and I will tear that golden hair out by the roots and wrench those blue eyes from their sockets. I will take my axe and chop the bitch into a million pieces, and then I will throw those pieces into a midden and send the pigs to feed on them...

"About you, of course. Would you like to see?"

"Perhaps we would all like to see," said my mother, leaning down from her high seat with icy curiosity.

Aphrodite took out her mirror and held it up. "Look, then."

I saw her by the pool, seated, and Actaeon beside her. He had quite a different expression on his face then the one he had when he was talking to me. It was bashful, coy. She was holding his hand and stroking it like a little mouse.

"Tell me, Actaeon, are you really in love with my half sister Artemis?"

"I have told her so," he said evasively.

Aphrodite pouted and widened her eyes. "I see. Well, it is good for a man to show loyalty, but tell me truthfully, would you not prefer me, if you had the choice?"

Actaeon looked wary; I saw that he was beginning to sweat. "I would not presume to choose between goddesses," he said, sounding like a diplomat walking a dangerous line in some royal court.

"Lucky Artemis," cooed Aphrodite. "Alas, her fortune is my sorrow. For I fell in love with you as soon as she described you to me. Alas, what delights I could offer you if only you were not already... taken." And she accompanied this with such a look of sweet yearning, twisting a tendril of her golden hair around her rosy finger, that no man could have resisted.

He looked at her, and his mouth fell open a little. "As to that..." he said slowly, "to be honest, Artemis is the first goddess I ever met in the flesh, and I was so overawed that perhaps I was a little hasty in my affections. And then, at first she disguised herself. When she appeared in her true form I admit that it was a shock, but one has to be polite, especially to a goddess."

"So perhaps there is hope for me after all?" whispered Aphrodite with a tremulous smile.

He knelt at her feet – he had never knelt at mine like that. "Goddess, there is no comparison between you. If you truly wish to bestow your love on me, humble mortal that I am, it would be far more than I deserve."

She smirked. "Indeed it would."

I saw his face turn ashen. I think he knew then the mistake that he had made. He clutched at her knee as she got up (or rather floated), and would have said more, but found himself grasping empty air.

Aphrodite turned to me with a raised eyebrow and pretty pout. "You see sister, what would you do without me to sort the wheat from the chaff, the glass from the diamonds? Men – they are such beasts, are they not?"

I looked at her, and felt myself turning red and mottled. There were titters of amusement. Athena, who does not like Aphrodite as a rule, laid her hand on my shoulder.

"Pay her no attention, she just hates to think that there is a man in the world who does not pine for her. Poor thing, she has little else to trouble her empty head about."

I pushed her off with a curse, and ran to my own rooms, hearing the laughter behind me. As it happened, the next day was the day that Actaeon and I usually met in the forest. I was tempted not to go. I would die rather than give him the idea that two goddesses were fighting over him. He was only a mortal, and not worth it. I was afraid, too, that he would see the shame under my anger when I confronted him. But then I thought to myself, I am a goddess, and he is nothing but a mortal boy. Why should I be afraid of him?

So I went to the forest, and there he was, as always sitting by the pool, eating something he had brought with him – a package of cheese and bread, or the like. He looked up when he saw me, and I couldn't believe my eyes – he looked me brazenly in the face, with the delight he showed always on first seeing me, and sprang up.

"Artemis! The week has seemed long to me since I saw you last. I have missed you..."

"I am sure you have," I said, with all the cold fury I could pull together. He looked at me, and his face fell.

"Is something wrong? Are you upset? Have they done something to hurt you, up there?"

The insolence of it, that he thought himself fit to console an immortal! I nearly lopped off his head where he stood, but that would been too good for him. "I will give you half an hour's start," I said. "And then I will set my hounds after you. Let us see how fast you can run, Actaeon. It had better be swift."

He stared at me, stupefied, as if he could not believe what I was saying. But I scowled back steadily, and put into my stare the full force of my divinity. An angry goddess is not a pretty sight – well, I was not a pretty sight even in a good mood. My eyes flashed like sheet lightning, and my body was outlined in an unearthly glare. He opened his mouth to say something, and then he ran.

I gave him half an hour, and then I set the wolf pups after him, and followed them myself, my bow at the ready. He was a fast runner, and he ran back in the direction of his own home – I guess he thought that if he could reach the edge of the forest he might escape me. But no one can escape a god. At length the wolves had him, bailed up with his back against a tree, their teeth ripping at his tunic and his hands as he tried to fend them off. He was screaming to me, pleading for mercy, but I ignored him and drew an arrow from my quiver. I pulled the string of the bow back as far as it would go – although the distance between us was short – and loosed it. It pinned him to the tree, straight through the heart. Even so, he still lived and struggled to breathe.

I could not resist. I strode up to him, and grabbed a handful of his hair at either side of his face, pushing his head back against the tree.

"This is your reward for being faithless to a goddess. Are you sure that you prefer my sister Aphrodite now?"

You will forgive me. I was young, and stupid, and could not keep my mouth shut.

He looked at me blankly with his beautiful river green eyes. "I never met your sister Aphrodite."

"Liar!" Overcome with fury, with a pain in my heart that must have worse than his, I grasped the arrow that stood in his chest and ripped it out of his flesh. He fell to the ground, bathed in blood, face down in those very leaves that we had lain in so often kissing and cooing.

I went back to my mother's Palace, and for a long time I came not again to the forest. I could not bear it. After a while the whispers died down and it seemed that everybody had forgotten the incident, except me. But I never went to sleep at night without seeing those wide green eyes, fixed on my face in horror and... hurt?

Some time later, in the morning, Athena came to me, her long red hair loose over her shoulders, and bent over my bed. She had a heavy face, sultry and secretive, but now I could see that it was full of pity and regret.

"Aphrodite lied to you. She's been telling us all for weeks what a good joke it was that she played on you. She never saw the boy – Actaeon, did you say his name was? She went to the forest but he was not there, so she made up a tale, just to spite you."

"But I saw his face, I heard him speak –"

"She had one of her friends – Nereia, I think it was - take on his part, to trick you."

I stared at her, aghast. And then I realised that of course Actaeon would not have been in the forest on that day, the day that she said she came to him. For he went there only one day in each week, and that was to meet me. All the other days he spent on his estate, doing whatever business mortals do. I thought of his expression when I changed my form, the hesitation, the thoughtfulness. There had been no shock or disgust – he had spoken the truth when he told me that he liked me just as I was.

I said nothing to Aphrodite, that foul bitch. I had been shamed enough; I didn't want to relive my humiliation. But after Actaeon, I never had a man again. And I never transformed again myself for a man's benefit. I was myself, broad and brawny and plain, and from now on, the world could like it or lump it.

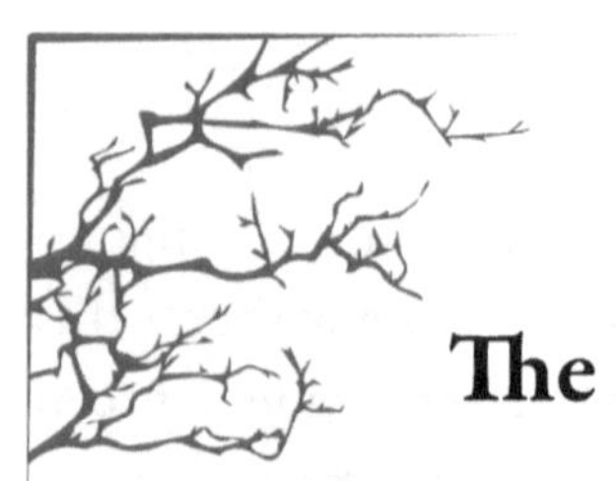

The Rainbow prince

He's a changeling, but doesn't know it.

This is not my baby, says his mother, closing her arms and turning away.

"We all feel that way at first," lies the nurse, hiding her misgivings, "You'll feel differently once you get used to one another."

The mother knows she'll never get used to him. His eyes are as bright and brown as a bush creature's, and his ears are much too delicate, flat to his head on its little stalk of a neck. He has an arcane beauty. She feeds him reluctantly, wonders if her milk will tame the faerie in him.

He hears his people singing to him as he sleeps at night, faint through the closed window. Their voices are sharp like pine needles. He knuckles his almond-shaped eyes, and whimpers in a world that doesn't belong to him.

The mother becomes attached to her elf baby. He grows as a human child, but he's slow to learn to read, his teachers say. He loves to kick a ball and watch comics on tv, but it's all a second language to him. You can see that in the shy way he dips his head when strangers approach, in the distance he keeps from others, in his wonder and confusion at the strangeness that surrounds him. Through the rice-paper wall that divides the boy and his adopted world, they perceive one another dimly, a shadow play.

The elf prince grows, and becomes a man, tall and beautiful. He finds a human mate. Sometimes, she imagines she sees his skin shifting colour like a rainbow reflected in moving water. He's as warm as hot springs, cool as cloud shadows. You think you have him safe in your arms, she thinks, but all you really have is a borrowed coat, left behind and smelling faintly of its last owner.

In time, the old ones draw him back amongst his own kind, having undergone his apprenticeship. Everything makes sense to him. He's a foreigner no longer. His own mother plaits his long silver hair. He misses the human world, slow and plain as it is. Sometimes he reaches out across the dimensions with his tendril fingers, and touches the forehead of his wife as she dreams of him, her rainbow prince.

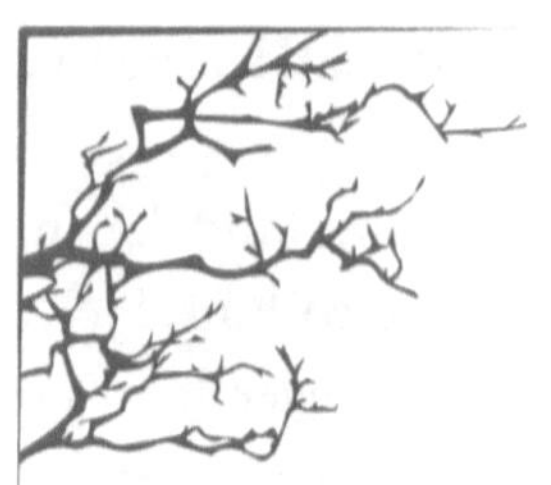

The Last Man

There were six of us. Me, and five women. There were only two in the Garden of Eden, and yet those two managed to spawn humanity. Why shouldn't we, then?

The women spent much of the day tending to the crops they'd coaxed, here in this place, untouched by the dust and the flame. This tiny rift in the hills, hidden from the searing winds, blessed with good soil and mild winters. Why? I have no explanation for this. Perhaps it was, literally, a Garden of Eden - a place of refuge designated by God, in which he could conduct His second experiment, after the first had failed.

In the old days I'd sometimes fantasised about this very scenario – being the only man left in a world of women. And here I was – me and them. I say women, but two were infants and one had not yet reached puberty. It was great. I didn't have to prove my manhood with my wallet. I didn't have to envy those guys born with even teeth and swinging shoulders and snake hips. I didn't even have to pretend to listen. I was all they had, and they better appreciate me.

But for me, the human race would dwindle and die, right here, right now. The women - Karen, Juanita and this dark chick whose name I couldn't pronounce - knew that, and treated me as careful farmers treat their only bull. No hunting and roaming for me: no sir, I stayed safe in the camp, while the women went gathering for my supper. If I didn't survive, no one was going to. I might have been one of those big cats in the zoo that used to be on the news before it happened - you know, the last Siberian tiger or whatever. Breed in captivity or perish. I didn't mind captivity, though, not a bit.

But there was one thing that I knew and they didn't. If they ever cottoned on, I'd be done for. One day, sooner or later, they'd notice that despite the nightly couplings - the dutiful, frantic, purposeful pounding and grunting and squirming - nobody was pregnant. So I used my spare time - and I had plenty of that - to think about what I'd say, when the inevitable questions were asked. Any excuse would do for a while, except the true one.

You see, before the world fell apart, I'd had a vasectomy.

You'd say - my vanished mates, whose voices I still hear in my dreams - what have you got to complain about? And it was true, I had more sex than I knew what to do with, and it was gloriously free – I didn't have to pay for dinner or mow the lawn or fix the deck. Apocalypse had its advantages. For once, eggs were in over-supply and sperm - well, there was just one store left that sold it, ladies, and those little wrigglers were as precious as pearls.

Before the fall, my feminist friends used to carry on as if a world without men would be a paradise, and they couldn't wait until we all died. Well, we *did* all die – except for me - and look what came to pass. I'd have laughed my head off, if I wasn't so nervous.

But, you know, it wasn't too bad. After all the fire and fury, the sky was blue, the birds sang - at least, what was left of them - and the love was on tap. It was a paradise, of sorts, and no God to order me out of it. I had it made, really.

Until *he* came. Out of the woods. Eighteen or so, handsome – even I could appreciate that – and virile. He came upon the camp when no one was there but me. He was thin – he'd obviously been fending for himself - and not very clean.

I don't know how he'd survived, nor how he'd found us. I knew for a fact that the world outside our valley was scorched and barren, a thousand miles of ash-grey death. Beyond that, more of the same.

But somehow out of this desolation he'd managed to find the one, last refuge of the species, God's little afterthought. He saw me, and held out his hands in the universal gesture of those in need of help. He wanted shelter and food. He wept to see a human face; I guess it must have been a while.

I came forward with a smile and took him by the elbow. I was much stronger than he, though with food and care, he would fill out and our positions would be reversed. I led him gently towards the hut that the women had constructed from me and gave him a meal of yams, and water. While he was eating, I went to get the axe.

I buried the young man in the pit we'd dug for shitting purposes and filled in when it was full. The smell of him, if it rose, would surprise no one.

Now, I was once more the only male, and the human race was doomed. I admit, I didn't care. I survived; that's a man's purpose, when you come down to it. You can't blame me for trying.

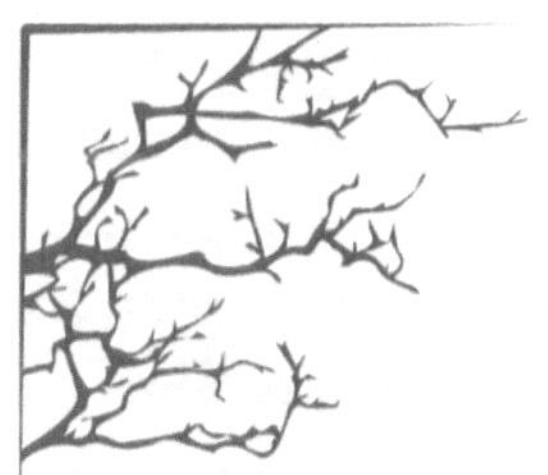

Valkyries

"I tell you, Reinhold, it was hell. Not war, but hell on earth, Satan amongst us."

Reinhold raised an eyebrow. "Really, my dear Conrad?"

"I don't say this lightly. If there were a place where – where sinners are sent to suffer torment for all eternity, this, *this* would be the place. Ypres, the winter of 1914."

"Surely you're exaggerating. You speak as if your experience were unique, as if this war were different from all other wars, but you know perfectly well that war is a constant of the human experience. There is nothing supernatural about it."

"We've both been in battle, Reinhold, we've both fought and seen death. But this... grinding, purposeless slaughter, the relentlessness of it, I've never experienced anything like it."

Reinhold lit a cigarette, and regarded me out of weary, pouched eyes. "Very well then, you'd better tell me about it. I can see you're going to, whether I want to hear it or not."

He laughed, and coughed behind his hand. War had left its mark on him too.

"You've heard it from others, I know," I began. "The mud, the filth – we lived in it day and night, we ate in it, slept in it. We waded up to our waist in the muck of decayed corpses, ate rats that were fat with feasting on our comrades, breathed the stink of foul water and smoke and poison gas...it was unspeakable. But I won't dwell on that...

I tell you, it was almost a relief to be ordered at last out of our trenches and towards the enemy lines. I led my company over the top at a run, as commanded, and of course the firing began at once. Half of us were mown down in the first 50 yards, and the air was dark with smoke and choking filth. They called me an officer, but after the first, I was scarcely leading the men; we were just running like a herd of beasts across the flaming field, trying to avoid the shells, deafened by the noise of death. I could not see far in front of me, but when I looked about, all that met my eyes was a grey ruin of mud and fire. And then, out of that Inferno, they came. *She* came."

Reinhold tapped his cigarette ash into the ashtray. Characteristically, he gave no sign that my words had affected him in any way. I could see that he didn't believe me.

She told me that it would be so. She told me that if I related what I saw that day with my own eyes, my fellows would think me mad. But I can't help it. That day is seared into my memory, and the only way to forget – no, not forget, I could never do that – recover, then, is to find someone, anyone, who will just listen. Who will just *hear.*

"By this time I was wounded," I went on. "Shrapnel had pierced my right leg, and I was weak from loss of blood. I tried to keep going, but my leg betrayed me, and I collapsed face-down in the red mud. I think that for a short while I lost consciousness.

I woke to find that the infernal noise of the shells and the guns and the screams of dying men had stopped. I wondered if I had died. The dead were all around me. Shrouded in grey, the battlefield was silent. As if time had paused, right there amongst it all. As if the world had taken a breath, and held it, and held it..."

"And then?" Reinhold drawled.

I should have known that he would not take me seriously. But he was my best friend. If I could not convince him to listen to me, then who would? Eleanor had left me months ago; now she was engaged to another man. I did not blame her. I was a wreck.

"I rolled myself over and began to drag myself through the churned earth. I am ashamed to say that I crawled back towards our own lines – at least, I think they were ours, but I was in such a state that if I had wandered into the English lines by mistake, I'd probably have thanked God for my deliverance."

Reinhold nodded, avoiding my eyes. Perhaps this raised painful memories for him: he too knew what it was to struggle wounded and alone among the slain.

"I was crawling, dragging myself along the ground, when I heard a noise of rushing wings – as if a flock of giant ravens were descending upon the dead. So naturally I looked up, and the sky was full of them."

I paused. I thought, if I end my story here, Reinhold will not think me mad, as so many others have done. But my story, ended here, would have no point. Reinhold tilted his head, listening, and this decided me.

"I saw women, on horseback, sweeping through the sky, their dark hair streaming behind them like storm-clouds. The beat of those huge wings, I can still hear it, the slow crash of waves upon a foul shore..."

"Women..." Reinhold's gaze became distant. "And were they...beautiful? Or are we talking about the hags of hell?"

Reinhold is an authority on women; he uses them, and calls it love.

"Beautiful? They were – beautiful in the way that a storm is beautiful, though it breaks your ship on the sea and flings you home to the four winds. Their faces were pale and fierce. Their hair was long and tangled, their eyes were like corpse lights..."

"How poetic, my dear fellow."

I ignored him. "I still remember them, glowing as they swept through the darkness, lit with a kind of pale, bluish fire, like gas ignited, and in their expressions an unholy joy. They swooped over the battlefield, empty of all save corpses, and wheeled again and again on the winged beasts, leaning down over the withers to sweep the ground with their terrible eyes. And then..."

I stopped and gulped at the whiskey with which Reinhold had kindly supplied me. The memory still turns me cold to my core.

"And then they came down, noisome, hurrying, like crows to a feast, and began to pick at the dead. Yes, pick at them as if their flesh was soft as hung game. I saw one of the women holding a thigh bone to her open jaws, gnawing at it with pointed teeth as we would a wish bone."

Reinhold's expression registered distaste. "Go on."

"I was afraid to move, but I did not want them to think me dead, either, and pluck me apart for a meal. So I just lay there, watching, trying to sink into the mud. And then she saw me.

I thought my last hour had come. I put my arms up to shield my face. I cowered – there was no courage left in me – and I cried out mercy, please, don't take me, I'm alive!

Her horse landed beside me – real as you are now – and stamped and snorted, the way mortal horses do. She swung herself down. There was no saddle nor bridle. She crouched beside me, and I nearly died then of sheer terror. Let those who speak of fear understand that a man can be brave, and yet under the right conditions, possessed by fear as by a demon that controls his very soul. I threw myself back from her, and scrabbled at the earth as if trying to dig myself a grave to hide in, and she spoke to me.

Her voice was low and full of contained ferocity.

"So you are alive, brave warrior, when all your comrades are dead upon this field. Are you not ashamed?" I could scarcely reply – my teeth were chattering and my body had turned to water – but I thought that there might be a shred of hope for me. She had not killed me yet, after all, nor plucked off a limb, so I forced myself to answer.

"I'm no coward, lady of the battlefield. But I have a wife at home, family. Let me live to go back to them. Please?"

At this she laughed, her full red mouth wide open and her head flung back into the sky.

"Why should I? Don't you want to join your comrades, warrior?"

"They are dead and I am yet alive," I got out. "Aren't there enough corpses for you, lady?"

She grinned again, and bent down. I was sure that my moment had come. To her I was merely carrion. But I felt myself being lifted up bodily, as lightly as one would lift a dead rabbit.

"Come with me, and see where the warriors go."

She flung me over the neck of her horse and then, before I could struggle – not that I had the strength – we had lifted up into the air and the wind was slicing past my head. I could feel her dreadful claws gasping the nape of my neck so that I did not fall. We rode faster, faster, the clouds an icy blur. I heard a wail of triumph and cruelty, whether from the lady or her sisters I couldn't tell, and fell back into unconsciousness.

"My God!" Reinhold leaned forward. I had managed to pique his interest, at least. "A nightmare, my friend. And – then you woke up safe in your hospital bed?"

I shook my head

"And then I awoke. I was in a place – how shall I describe it? It was like – like a kind of cathedral, all arches and towers and pillars reaching high as the eye could see. But there was something pallid and grim about this building...after a while I saw that everything within it was constructed from bones, save the windows. Those were matted with cobwebs, and almost lightless. They reminded me of dead men's eyes, open on a world they cannot see. I could scarcely breathe, the place smelled like the back of a butcher's shop, where the offal is discarded for the dogs."

"This place – it is built from the bones of the dead?" I asked her.

"Yes indeed. It is built from the bones of those you call cannon fodder, the commoners, bread and wine of the sword. Your friends did not die in vain. But the warriors – the true warriors – they do not share the common fate."

And then she took me outside the great doors, made of the stretched skins of the victims of war, and I saw a line of men, shackled to each other, moving slowly along the dusty road. Their heads were downcast, their backs scored by the marks of the whip.

"Who then are these?"

The lady laughed, and her laugh was like the cry of a crow.

"They are the great of this world. They go to the quarry, where they will clean and carve and polish the day's takings. They will work there till night falls, and then they will return to sleep in the charnel pit we have made for them."

She gestured, and I saw beside the cathedral, a deep pit sloping away, and within it lay those parts of a man that hang upon his bones – organs, arteries, meat and blood, all forming an indescribable soup of putrescence. I could not see how anyone could survive, let alone sleep, in such a noxious stew. But then, these men were not really alive.

I heard the crack of the whip, and my attention was borne back to the chain gang. Beside them stood two women, of the kind who had brought me, naked but for a thick leather belt around the waist - enough to hold a whip, a sword and a flask. The whips looked to be rawhide - made of human flesh, I didn't doubt. All things in this place were made of the leavings of the dead.

"You see the general there, how he bleeds and stumbles? The common folk – you and your like – their bones go to make our halls. But those that lead you into war, and make their plans, and sit upon the hilltop ordering all things – *those* labour for us, for all eternity. All the greatest warriors are here with us, here."

She stopped, and raised her hand and set up a great shout. "Hey there, Bonaparte!"

A man looked up at the sound of his name, and his eyes were those of an animal who has been beaten, and beaten again, and now only hopes for death. Despite the face, covered with the white dust of bones, and the broken curve of his spine, I thought that I recognised the conqueror of Austerlitz, the defeated leader of Waterloo.

"Alexander?"

One of the women spat her whip out into the line, and caught a man around the waist. He was young in years, but ancient in suffering. His body had the marks of many cuts, and his feet were swollen with bruises. But those famous, farseeing eyes, blue and wide, still gazed out, as empty as one of the busts that were all that was left of him.

The woman turned to me, shaking out her long, tangled hair, acrid as ash.

"What would you rather be, warrior – the bricks or the builder?"

She saw the answer in my eyes, and bared her teeth in a show of humour.

"Valhalla is not ready for you yet, little soldier. Come back when you can make yourself useful."

She leaned forward, and picked me up again with one mighty hand. And then she flung me from her. Darkness took me. I felt myself falling as if from a massive precipice. And this time I woke, as you said, in hospital, in Dresden, with a pretty nurse leaning over me and wiping my brow with a damp cloth."

Reinhold was silent for a moment, and then he looked at me, one side of his mouth lifted in a sceptical smile.

"So, to summarise, you were taken to the hall of the Valkyries - perhaps we can call it Valhalla? - and warned of the fate that awaits all soldiers killed in battle. Or worse, their leaders. An interesting allegory. But, Conrad, you don't really believe it all happened, do you?"

I held out my hands. In the palm of each was stamped an eye, in blistered flesh.

"The eye of Odin. She branded me, and told me to remember her. I tell you, Reinhold, Hell is no pit of endless fire. Hell is that cathedral, and that chain gang, and those women... I shall not go to war again."

Reinhold examined my palms, fingering the brands curiously, and then placed my hands back upon my knees. "I see. And you feel you must find someone who believes you, lest this tale go with you to your deathbed. Well, I believe you, my friend. Some things are... beyond our understanding."

"You believe me?" I was startled, but relieved.

"Yes." He reached within his shirt, and pulled out a chain. On the end of this chain – silver I think – was an eye, made of bone. "You see, I too have a tale to tell – but of love, than war."

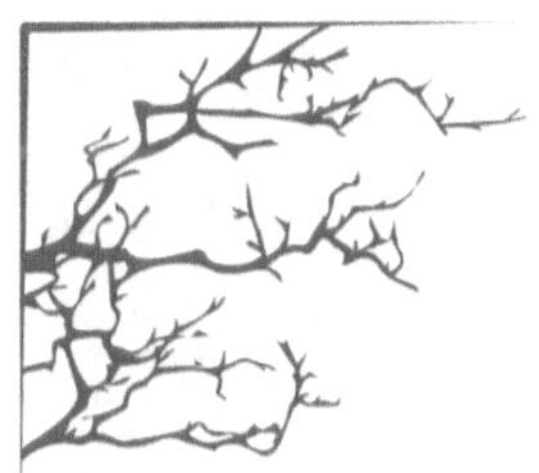

The Wind

Fifty years ago the river flowed deep and brown between steep banks, the glint of fish and the glitter of gum leaves shimmering under summer rain. Under the mud of a thousand rotted trees, the bones of a million small lives, the still slow silence of the black cold depths, the wind rested.

Now the river is a trickle; the fish lie gasping in fetid pools, the unrelenting sun burns the river bed to a snakeskin pavement of cracked earth, and the thirsty farmlands stretch away to either side, their cotton and their fruit trees withered away. There is no more water to steal.

Beside the dead river stands a farm house. It belonged to Emily's grandfather, and now she's here, gathering what's left of his life. Peeling weatherboard, yellowed curtains, a long verandah looking over what used to be a garden. A few deep-rooted trees, a small, empty dam: a rain water tank holds enough for a few days' stay.

It's not hard work. By early afternoon, Emily's packed the dusty kitchen utensils and plates into a cardboard box for the thrift shop, and put the contents of the wardrobe and drawers - flannelette shirts, work-stained trousers, blue singlets and threadbare underclothes - into garbage bags. It's one of those autumn days that's not too cold, not too hot, the sky a cornflower blue, so she sits out on the verandah, puts her feet on the old wooden rail, and looks down towards the river bed.

As the evening fades in, the wind rises, gentle as an old woman. It caresses the bleached paddocks, brushes the tops of the gum trees with its dry lips, curls around the house and slides over the tin of the roof, sighing. Emily feels the first chill of winter's kiss, faint around her collarbone. A flurry of tiny birds lifts from the dirt of the yard and wheels away, cloud-wise.

It's time to go in. She closes the old wooden door, thinks about locking up, doesn't. This place is a long way from anywhere, at the end of a track it takes her half an hour to drive down, and then there's only more sepia farmland and a road to nowhere much, a few skinny sheep looking in puzzlement up at her as if to say, where did you come from?

Once the sun's down, there's a bite in the air, so she decides to light the fire. She makes a small teepee out of newspapers she found stacked in the shed - some going back to the 1930s - and twigs, and holds a match to them. The chimney sucks greedily at the flames. She hopes there are no bird's nests in there, after all this time unused.

Once she has the fire lit, she sits before it, in her grandfather's beat-up rocking chair, and listens to it hiss and chew. Outside, the wind rattles the door like a stranger in the night. Her grandfather's ghost, she thinks with an irrational shiver - and then shrugs it off and makes herself a cup of tea.

That night she dreams that dark, wet shapes swirl on the wind, that the night sky flows like water in flood, poison green, fungus yellow. She dreams that the wind scuttles under the eaves, and slithers through the cracks and crevices of the house, heavy as pestilence. She opens her eyes to the dawn breaking pale through her window, and in her muddled half-sleep, she sees the trees leaning in towards her, like a warning.

She blinks out from the bed clothes for half an hour, uneasy and cold, then slides back to sleep.

Later, she makes strong coffee and takes it outside. The wind has dropped to a murmur, picking lightly at her hair. The dregs of the cup are bitter, so she goes to the rail to throw them out, and her eye catches on a scattering of ragged shapes below. It's the birds, the tiny round-bodied finches she saw in the yard the day before, but they're all dead, their tiny feet stiff as kindling, their feathers oddly luminous.

She steps carefully down the stairs - the timber's half-rotten - and squats down for a closer look. She can't imagine what could have killed them all, thirty or more, all at once. There's no sign of injury, just a greenish pallor that reminds her of fridge mould. She picks up their tiny feathery bodies with dishwashing gloves and puts them in a plastic shopping bag, feeling sickened. If God sees a single sparrow fall and grieves, how about thirty?

She cleans the house, scrubbing down fifty years of neglect. Thank God it was outside, down by the river, where he did it - she couldn't have brought herself to clean up bloodstains, let alone stay alone in a house where someone had killed himself. She tries to remember him in happier times, pottering around the yard, but she's beginning to understand how he must have felt, in his later years. There is something ominous about this place, something more than lonely.

As night falls, the wind begins to rise again. She thinks she hears voices, hissing, snarling. They sing of cattle trampling the land like giant locusts, and starving by stagnant pools. They sing of fat green fields fed on the river's blood, while far below, the great lightless lakes drain to deserts. They sing of dark water and darker futures.

She hurries to light the fire, and sits close to it as she can, as primitive humans used to, for protection more than warmth. Behind the clouded glass of the firebox, something scrabbles and claws in the shaft. Just metal expanding in the heat, she tells herself, peering into the flames.

There's no TV out here, so she opens a book she brought, resolutely reads it, despite the fear scratching at her shoulder. It's just a wind, she tells herself, just a wind. Still, she gets up and locks the door, against what, she doesn't know. Outside, it lifts and grows, wrapping itself around the flimsy walls, making the fire flicker and leap. She hears it crying up from the river, a whining, warning sirens' song of dread and invitation.

She can't stand it, just sitting there, with the night scrabbling outside. She gets up, opens the door, finds it torn from her and flung wide, and then there's a thud and a snap, and a body lands at her feet. Emily jumps and screams - but it's just a possum that's fallen down from the roof. It's young, and very dead. Its round eyes stare at nothing, blank and shining.

The wind drops. But the air has a strange smell, noxious and sharp at the same time, acid on carrion. She looks down at the dead possum: its fur glows faintly, greenly. The verandah railings are coated in a luminous frost. She shuts the door quickly, and piles more wood on the fire.

This time, when she goes to bed, Emily makes sure that the door is locked and that all the windows are shut and bolted. Even so she can't get to sleep. The wind chants and mutters, weaving a spell of black mud and dead trees, poison water and sour air. She stares out, all the long night, at the square of window, and imagines that the dry river is rising, spreading its dark waters up over the bare paddocks and over the rotten steps. It carries the bones of birds and trees, cattle and kangaroos. It calls to her.

In the morning she buries the possum in the long-gone garden, and loads the boxes and bags into the car. She walks down to the river and stands on the cracked mud, no sign of any flow here, not even a puddle of standing water.

In the bright autumn sun, the last night's imaginings seem absurd. She thinks about calling Tim, her boyfriend, about asking him to come out and spend the last night with her here. There are still a few things to wrap up before the real estate agent comes to value the place, and she'd rather not be alone again, in the dark. But really - why not? It'd be pretty hard to explain on the phone, and anyway, there's no mobile reception, she'd have to drive for miles in hopes of picking up a signal. One more night. It won't kill her.

This time she locks herself in before the sun dims, and turns all the lights on, and sets the fire, and sets up her ipod dock to play something cheerful and shallow. But through it all, under the music and behind the light and flame, there's an underlay of ill-intent, a low, warning note that seems meant for her ears only. Emily decides not to go to bed, after all, but to stay by the fire, under the unblinking gaze of the electric light. Tomorrow she will leave, drive back to the city, get her mind in order.

But in the small hours, when the fire is low and red, a soft voice snatches at the door, snuffles at the timbers. She wakes with a start, in the old rocking chair, and thinks she hears it whining, the words from a fairytale she remembers from childhood.

Let me in, let me in, little pig, or I shall huff and puff and blow your house down.

She pulls the blankets around her and wrenches open the door to the fire box. She grabs cut logs and stuffs them into the coals, then newspaper, to make them catch, until fire bursts forth red and hot on to the hearth. She backs away as it eats up the old coir hearth-rug, and begins to blacken the floorboards, seeking out the cracks between them. She watches, her back to the door, as it climbs her grandfather's settee and sweeps up the yellow net curtains. The heat forces her out on to the verandah, not dark now, but washed in seething red. She stumbles down the steps and they disintegrate behind her. She runs down towards the river in her night things, dropping the blanket in the yard.

When she gets to the river bank, the red light from the house illuminates a torrent, a roaring flood of darkness. She glances back and sees the sky roiling with colour, corpse green, neon-blue, poison yellow, and flames rushing over the dry grass towards her like a pack of hungry wolves. Sparks catch on her hair, smoke blinds her, and the black river surges up towards her bare feet.

The wind gathers her up like new-killed veal, and the river opens its mouth to receive.

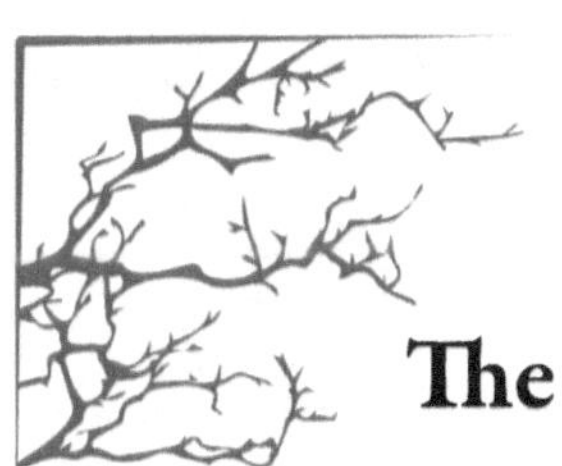

The Sculpture Garden

"You ready for this?"

"Sure, beam us down, Scotty. How do I look?"

"Cute, but that's not what I pay you for."

"You haven't paid me yet."

"I wouldn't worry too much about that," said Scotland Terminal dryly. "If we pull this off, neither of us will ever have to work again."

Tosca, alighting from the shuttle pad to a vista of sweeping lawns, vast tennis courts and a prehistoric mansion that looked like it covered about one third of the planet, had to agree. Verrucas Vanderbilk clearly wasn't short of a dollar – and he'd certainly rolled out the red carpet for them.

Literally. They walked down the crimson pathway with their thumbs casually looped in their belts, like consummate professionals, but it was hard not to feel overawed – not so much by the magnificence of their surroundings, but by what stood in them.

"Is that what I think it is?" asked Tosca in a low voice, jerking her head towards a marbled mass to the left.

"Yep. A triple-headed chimera, the last of its kind. And that – ", he pointed to a small group of rock-like structures, "is a family of tree-elephants from Greater Plutonium. Extinct now. Just about all these things are."

"What a shame." Tosca stared, round-eyed, at a Three-Clawed Bandersnatch posed arrestingly by the broad front steps. "Still, I guess it's one way of preserving them for posterity, huh? What's he do, stuff them, or something?"

"He's got a basilisk. Point, aim, fire – and there's your sculpture. Neat, ain't it?"

"But I thought they were..."

"Extinct. They are. He's got the only one."

Just then, a flaccid, custard -like substance flowed down the steps.

"Welcome! Mr Terminal, it's great to finally meet you! I see you've been admiring my menagerie, ha ha! Why, that's nothing, just you wait till you see what I've got inside. And Mademoiselle? Enchanted!"

The semi-liquid mass hovered over Tosca's hand for a moment. She shuddered.

"Now," the billionaire collector explained as he led them into the house and melted onto a purpose-built air-seat. He motioned to his guests to do the same. "I understand that you're the best trophy hunter the galaxy has to offer – and that's exactly why I've brought you here. As you can see...," he waved towards the statue-infested grounds, "I have just about every extinct legend known to sentient beings. But there's one mythical creature that's managed to elude me – oh yes, I've employed dozens of hunters to go out and fetch me one, but all of them – all – have returned empty-handed and that is..."

"The rare and critically endangered unicorn of the Lesser Spiral Galaxy," finished Terminal, taking a large cheroot from the golden box offered him and sticking it thoughtfully in the corner of his mouth. "No one's been able to find one, let alone shoot it and bring it back. You sure it still exists?"

Vanderbilk smiled, or rather liquefied slightly around the mouth area. "It exists, by Jupiter, and I want it. I'm getting old, you know, and there's not much time left. Before I go, I want to have one of everything. Everything, I tell you. I want you to find that thing, shoot it, and bring it to me – and I want you to do it fast. Understood?"

"No problem." Terminal rose, and Tosca rose with him. "So, about the money. One million spacewads. Half now, half when I return with the beast." He held out a lean and calloused hand, but thought better of it when he noticed Vanderbilk preparing to extend his own amorphous appendage. "Deal?"

Vanderbilk nodded. "Deal."

Back in the Jeep, Tosca looked at him. "That guy is going to be mighty pissed if you don't come back with one of those things."

Terminal gave a laconic grin. "That's why I'm the best. I always get what I come for." He winked.

She shrugged, ignoring the come-on. "Oh yeah? Even you can't conjure a unicorn out of thin air."

"Nope, you're right there. That," said Terminal, punching in the coordinates of True Earth, "is your job."

Hovering above the faintly steaming atmosphere of the ancient planet, Tosca's heart sank. "We're not going to have to trek through all that, are we?"

"The scanning cameras will narrow it down for us. They'll identify any anomalous being emitting mystic energy, and then all we have to do is go and check it out on the ground."

Tosca looked doubtful. "It's awfully big, though."

"Sure, but there's a coupla things narrow it down. Beasts like this, see, they can't survive in jungle. So that rules out about two thirds of the planet. They don't like forest, neither – their horns get tangled. So that rules out most of the rest. Nah, what we're looking for is grassy, open plains. Like...that one, right there."

Tosca saw that the camera's live energy indicator had turned a pulsing neon blue as they skimmed low across the planet. It looked like there was something down there, sure enough. They set the Jeep to stationary float, pulled on their hazmat suits, and let themselves drift gently down through the atmosphere.

"Now what?" she asked, as they trudged through waist high tussocks towards a small running stream.

"Now we wait." Terminal looked meaningfully at Tosca. "This is where *you* come in. So I'll make myself scarce, and you might as well make yourself comfortable. You got everything you need?"

"Sure... But what if it decides to stick its horn right through my..."

"You *are* a virgin maiden, aren't you?"

Tosca looked indignant and patted the left side of her chest, which was flat as a board. "I'm an Amazon, from Artemis. What do *you* think?"

But Terminal had disappeared. All she could see were acres of windblown grass in every direction. She sank down, and crossed her legs.

The fading sun of True Earth had almost dipped to the horizon when she felt the earth trembling, and woke up with a start. Bending its graceful neck over her, as if inspecting a rare flower, the unicorn ruffled her hair with its perfumed breath. Its rheumy eyes were innocently inquiring, but the purple hairs on its muzzle were peppered with silver, and its flanks were scrawny. Clearly, it was an elderly animal.

She drew in her breath. "Come on," she said softly, "it's all right. Come to me."

The unicorn sank to its knees, wheezing, and then rolled over, its head resting on her upper thigh. Unicorns, by repute, live for 999 years; this one was clearly nearing the end of its lifespan. She stretched out her hand, and scratched its frayed ears. "Poor old thing," she said, "You're just like me, really. The only one left of your kind. We should stick together."

Abruptly, the unicorn kicked and screamed. With a sharp exclamation, Tosca scrambled up. "What the heck! How could you?"

"That's what we came here for," said Terminal, in a strangely cold voice. He looked down at the dead unicorn, his mouth twisting. "You know, sometimes I think it's time for me to quit this job."

Tosca bit her lip. Amazons don't cry, she told herself. "Well, I guess we might as well get it back to the Jeep."

They stood for a moment, looking down at the fallen beast in sombre silence; it was not the moment of triumph they had anticipated. Suddenly Terminal whirled around.

"What the heck is that?"

Announced by a barely noticeable rustling in the grass, two small creatures, about the size of antique hedgehogs, began to trundle towards the stream.

"Close your eyes!" Terminal yelled. Tosca squeezed her eyes tight shut, and in a moment felt him fitting a pair of tight goggles over her head. She opened them to find herself looking through a pair of dark reflective glasses.

"What is it?"

"Basilisks."

"But you said they're..."

"Extinct. I know. And you know why? Because they feed on the droppings of unicorns. No unicorns – no basilisks. That's why Vanderbilk owns the only one. Until now." With a swift pounce, he scooped the two little creatures up, and stuffed them into his carrier pouch, not forgetting a sample of unicorn poop for the M5 (Mythical Mammal Meal Manufacturing Machine). "You never know when they might come in useful," he said, and activated intra-atmospheric liftoff.

When Terminal and Tosca arrived back at the sumptuous headquarters of the billionaire, they were surprised to find that they were not the only visitors. The lawns were crowded with sentient beings of various shapes and sizes, many of them wearing a variant of the traditional garb of the trophy hunter, a cream-coloured safari suit and baseball cap. Vanderbilk came flowing forward, a sinuous smile wreathing his cheeks.

"Well done, well done! I'm now the only guy in the entire galaxy who can boast a unicorn – and I always will be, because this was the very last one. Imagine that - what a triumph! And to celebrate, I've invited every single collector and hunter of note here to my modest little hideaway, to witness my – our – astounding success. And now - let's create Art!"

A trolley bearing the covered corpse of the unicorn, arranged in a suitable pose with the aid of struts and wires, was ceremonially rolled through the crowd and placed on a custom-built platform. Vanderbilk whipped off the cover with a flourish, and bringing forth a small shuttered box, carefully pointed it towards the body in the manner of an ancient camera. In an instant, the dead flesh became gleaming stone; the assembled crowd clapped and hooted and stomped their cowboy boots.

"Would you like to say a few words?" Vanderbilk asked, turning to Terminal and Tosca.

Terminal grinned, and strolled up beside him. Tosca followed, clutching a glittery handbag.

"Sure," he said, creased blue eyes scanning the crowd like an Indian surveying a herd of buffalo, "But first, we've brought a little extra something to start the party. Tosca, release the basilisks, would you honey?"

Tosca opened her clutch bag. Two furry noses emerged from the glitter; two sets of beady eyes blinked in the light, and focused on five hundred curious, craning faces...

On the following day, Tosca and Terminal took their leave, together with an overflowing case of spacewads and the two basilisks, whom they had affectionately christened Basil and Rosemary.

"Goodbye, and thanks for having us." Terminal touched his hat to his host and the assembled guests.

Vanderbilk did not reply, nor did anyone else utter a word. But then, marble rarely does.

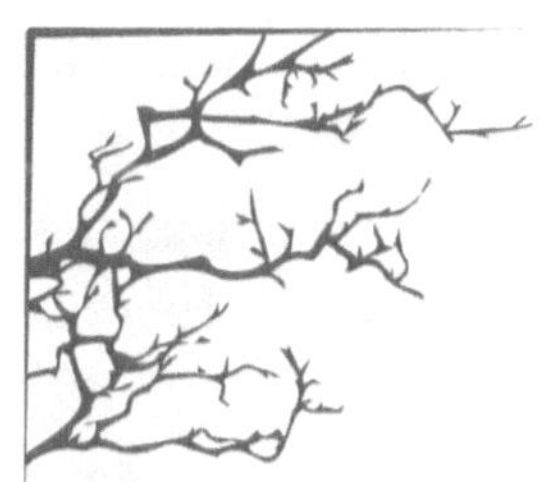

The Position

When I took over The Position things had pretty much gone to pot. There were rules - too many if you ask me, and half of them contradicting the other half - but no real enforcement. Just the constant *threat* of enforcement, and we all know that doesn't work.

"You've got to come down hard," I said to my Second in Command, who I'd kind of inherited, along with the rest of the staff.

"Oh we do, sir," says he, doing his best to lick my arse while not turning his back on the old guy, either. "We made it pretty clear what happens if you don't toe the line. Crystal clear, sir."

"Yes, but it generally helps if the punishment for the crime comes due *before* you're dead," I say tartly, and he falls silent. I know he doesn't like me, but there was a reason I was brought in. He knows that.

"And not only is there no stick," I go on, "but there's precious little bloody carrot either! You've got to encourage people, not just shout at them. First principle of good management, son."

He opens his mouth and shuts it. I know what he wants to say. "But we *do* encourage them, sir!"

Bollocks! Harps and choir practice? What school of marketing did *he* graduate from?

Well, it's time I set this house in order. First, the paperwork. I reckon the publication department's had way too much time on its hands. Bloated, too. So I call everyone together, and a ragtag lot they are too, with their frocks and overgrown beards.

"Why have we got...let's see, over fifty major compendiums of Regulatory Orders, and none of them consistent! No fish on Friday, no cows for some, no pigs for others, and what exactly is the problem with shellfish? Who wrote this drivel, anyway?"

"It's allegorical," pipes up a thin guy with straggly brown hair. "You can't just lay it out plain and simple, people won't understand. They like to hear stories, parables if you will..."

"Well you've clearly got a PhD in barmy lit," I say, marking the name tag down on my list for a redundancy offer. Jesus. Right. Last on, first off, as they say. "Where I come from, if we want somebody not to do something, we lay it out plain - Don't Do It."

He's still muttering gently into his bum fluff when some other character with a pot belly and a hooked nose pipes up.

"Yes indeed sir, and that is why we brought out the revised edition. It tells you everything you need to know, in detailed specifications, none of this parable nonsense. How much of your estate you should leave to your second cousin once removed, how many goats you should give your wife's mother after her third menstruation, the goat's that is not the –"

"Thank you for your contribution." I shut him up before he can climb any further up my backside. "I believe the approach you're describing is called micro-management. Now, I'm sorry to have to tell you all," (I'm not really) "that I'm looking at a significant downsizing operation. In future, we will be publishing once a millennium, with updates on the first Friday of each century - and it will be short and sharp. If you can't fit what you need to tell 'em in ten pages, you talk too much. No allegories, no by-laws and fine print. I want it to read like the instructions on the bus door. Pay your fare. Don't get off while we're moving. No drawing on the seats."

Mr Fine Print looks mighty pissed off. I think, here's one we should have escorted off the premises by five pm or there'll be trouble. So I have a quiet word to Security and Mohammed whatsisname disappears out the double glass doors with his cardboard box and photos of his four wives peeking out the top. No wonder he stays late at work, scribbling all that rubbish about virgins and raisins.

"You know they're lobbying to get the old Chief back," says Mavis as she puts out the evening roast. "They don't like all this new broom stuff."

"They'll like it even less tomorrow," I says, squeezing Mavis' bottom. "I've scrapped all the ramblings about sex being off limits. The Old Chief must have had erectile dysfunction, or dementia. Or maybe his missus looked like the back end of a cow."

Ah, tomorrow. All up, I've got about 1062 lightning strikes planned, all to be carried out at the same time, in an orderly manner, at 0900 hours. It's about time these people learned right from wrong, and there's nothing like a short sharp shock to teach them that. And of course, there'll be about the same number of goodie bags distributed. I'm told manna isn't a popular taste right now, so I've got the troops to pack up four hundred iPods instead, and some nice chocolates.

"Don't drop it *on* them," I made sure to tell the guys, "Just on the doorstep, or if they haven't got one, down beside the feet will do. And gently. You could take a tip from...who's that guy who got Salesman of the Year five hundred years running? Oh yes, Santa Claus. But no drinking on the job, capiche? That's what got him in the end...a very sad finale to a great career, if you ask me."

Capito. They were getting the idea, though the work attire was still a bit inappropriate. From underneath you could see right up those skirts, but, well, you can't tackle everything in the first week. Especially not the tackle.

And now for the fun bit. Mavis says it's a shame to kill for sport, but I tell her, it's for their own good in the long term. We'll pick a few bad ones out of the herd and you just wait and see how the stock improves over time. It's just common sense and good farming technique, not rocket science.

So I get out the high-powered lightning bolt bazooka with the telescopic sights, absolutely the latest weapon for this kind of thing, and right away I see a bunch of those runty, mean-tempered little buggers, conspiring away in some tepid nastiness under a big white monstrosity, and I let them have it. Sizzle, squeak, ker-splatt! Ten less troublemakers! This calls for a beer!

"Mavis! Mavis?"

Where is that bloody woman! While I'm waiting I pop off another twenty, just like that. I know you're not supposed to enjoy the work but to be frank and honest, it gives me a sense of enormous satisfaction. You can almost see the muddy waters of the gene pool clearing as the muck and debris are got rid of, as well they should be. In fact it strikes me that if I electrocuted a whole burrow - and these things usually stick out like a wart on a pig's backside, with flags on top and guards marching round and round the perimeter - I could clean the pool even quicker. It's an exciting thought!

"Mavis! Bring us a slab will you chook?" What's taking her so long?

Course, there are too many rotten apples to get rid of in just one season. But it's a start. Maybe plague would hurry the whole process up, or mixamotosis...but that's a bit indiscriminate. Now that was the Old Chief's mistake. The good ones caught it same as the bad - no one could work out whether it was him taking potshots or just bloody bad luck. Plus, the lousy ones lived to breed while the ones you wanted to multiply died off nobly or joined nunneries. Bad policy, that.

Anyway, looks like I'm going to have to get my own beer. This feminism thing has gone too far! So I gets up and makes a move towards the fridge when in trots Mavis, and she's brought a friend.

"This is Mary," she says, "from next door."

I look her over. Nice arse.

"Nice to meet you, darl."

"Mary is Jesus' mum," says Mavis primly.

I nod politely - and then the penny drops. The little fart I just sacked along with Mohammed and Joseph Smith and the rest of the bloody useless Publication Department. And hang on, weren't there rumours about The Chief and this Mary woman? So maybe Jesus is a chip off the old block...won't save him, though.

"I'm not rehiring him," I state flatly. "But I'll turn him off with a nice little package, you needn't worry about paying the bills.'" Because somebody told me she's a single mother, and I'm not some kind of ogre.

"I'm not worried about my boy," she says calmly. 'His heart wasn't really in it anyway. He wants to spend a lot more time surfing."

"Well then! This calls for a beer!"I exclaim, looking pointedly at Mavis.

"Actually, Mary and me and the other company wives, we've knitted something," says Mavis. "We thought it might come in handy."

So Mavis holds up one end and Mary holds up the other, and they spread the thing out like a bedsheet. And bless me if it isn't a banner.

"We thought you could trail it out from a plane, or an angel, or something," suggests Mary. "Like sky-writing. It's all they really need to know, and it might work better than, well, more severe methods..."

She trails off, and exchanges a glance with Mavis. Of course, like all women, they're soft as custard at heart. They don't realise that sometimes you have to be cruel to be kind. But there you are, that's the female of the species.

"**Play nice and share your toys**," says the banner, with lovely little curly bits in green and yellow - don't know how they managed it in the time – "**or you'll be sorry when your father gets home!**"

I can see Mavis thinks it's a bit of a joke, but Mary is deadly serious.

"People ought to pay more attention to their mothers," she tells me. 'If only Jesus had listened to my advice, a lot of trouble could have been avoided!"

And I suddenly realise, here - right under my nose - here are my perfect enforcers! Women! God's police! Why didn't I think of that!

Did you enjoy these stories?

For more stories and books by F.L.Rose, visit https://fallaciousrose.com/

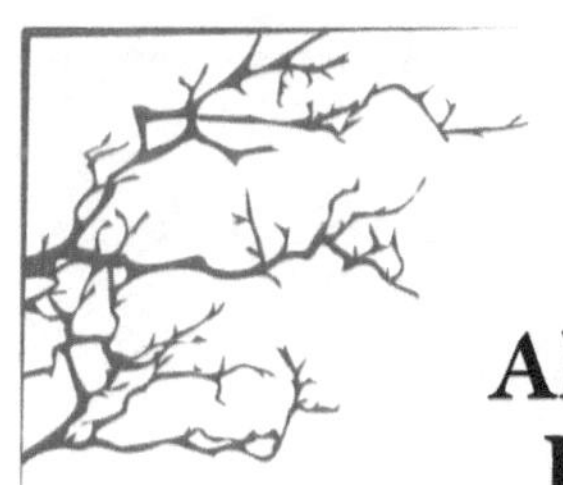

Also by F.L.Rose/ Fallacious Rose

The Point of Us

Paul, a Catholic school teacher, is losing his faith. His students couldn't care less about literature, and his teenage daughter has become unreachable. But when he signs up as a prison visitor to a notorious hitman, life becomes a whole lot more complicated.

Meanwhile Terentia, his wife, can't get a publisher for her latest book, Emma, the secretary at their daughter's school, discovers a problematic half-brother, and her husband, Dave, is accused of racism on the school bus run.

This is a story of four people suddenly forced to confront the purpose of their lives, who they are and what really matters. Is character, fate, or can people change?

Find out more[1]

Pandora's Jar

IT'S 531 AD. EMPEROR Justinian and his ex-prostitute Empress, Theodora, rule the eastern Roman Empire. In the sophisticated, complex world of the Byzantine Empire, power and death go hand in hand. But Anastasia, successful ex-courtesan of Constantinople, isn't interested in politics. Instead she plans to spend her retirement reading, entertaining friends and enjoying the sea air. However when her

---

1.   https://fallaciousrose.com/book/the-point-of-us/

much-loved protege Helena is raped and murdered, Anastasia sets out to seek answers – and revenge.

Pandora's Jar is a sexy, funny historical page turner you won't easily be able to put down...

Find out more[2]

A Portrait Under Water

A PORTRAIT UNDER WATER is a new take on the myth of Orpheus and Eurydice. It's a story of death, grief, and the unbreakable bonds of passionate love.

Eurydice's husband Orpheus, a well-known musician, disappears from a party boat in Sydney Harbour on his thirtieth birthday. Three days later police recover his drowned body. Desperate with grief, Eurydice tries to find a reason for his apparent suicide. The dead provide no answers, and the theories of friends and accusers – depression, obsessive love, a drunken accident – don't satisfy her.

Escaping a bitter, blaming mother in law and a morbidly curious press, Eurydice flees to Spain. There she explores the boundaries between life and death, but Orpheus is hard to reach. Wherever the dead may be, they don't speak our language there, and it's a long way off.

Find out more[3]

---

2.   https://fallaciousrose.com/book/pandoras-jar/

3.   https://fallaciousrose.com/book/a-portrait-under-water/

www.ingramcontent.com/pod-product-compliance
Lightning Source LLC
Chambersburg PA
CBHW031405160726
47993CB00003B/1117